Alive I Cried

Alive I Cried

Josh Webb and Rodey Webb

JS Publishing
South Carolina

Alive I Cried

All Rights Reserved Copyright © 2004 by Rodey Webb

Published in the United States of America
First Edition

No part of this publication may be reproduced or used in any form or by any means—graphic, electronic, or mechanical, including photocopying, recording, taping or information storage and retrieval systems—without the written permission of the publisher.

JS Publishing
7 Office Park Road
Suite 238
Hilton Head Island, SC 29928

Library of Congress Control Number: 2004111031
ISBN 0-9759999-0-7

Cover Art:
THOMAS CREASER
Pencil Etching on head stone, 18 x 24" (34 x 45 cm)

Cover and Book Design:
JUDE SHRINER

Printed in the United States of America

United Book Press
Baltimore, Maryland

Books may be ordered online:
www.joshwebb.com
rodeyww@hargray.com
www.jspublishing.com

Dedicated in loving memory of

Joshua James Webb

October 25, 1968—January 31, 1998

Acknowledgements

So many people lent their loving support during those endless, dark days. It was a great team effort, as Josh needed us all. Thank you is inadequate.

My appreciation, gratitude and heartfelt thanks to:

Julie
Jim and Betty
Jody
Judith
Leo & Mickey
Kathy, Patty, Laurie, Lisa and Lenny

Eleanor
Bud & Linda, Janet, Jerry & Diane, John & Carol
Sig Pi Fraternity Brothers
Ray & Linda and Phil & Jane
Kim & Jon, Dave & Carolyn, Char and Ellen
Reverend Steve
Sherburne-Norwich Community
Eileen

Special thanks to all the dedicated doctors, nurses and medical staff too numerous to name

CONTENTS

Prologue   xi

Introduction: Beginnings   15

Chapter 1—**Sermons to Myself**   21
Josh Webb

Chapter 2—**From Bed to Bedside**   37
Josh Webb

Chapter 3—**A Mother's Perspective**   59
Rodey Webb

Chapter 4—**Donor Experience**   70
Julie Webb

Chapter 5—**Relapse**   81
Josh Webb

Chapter 6—**ICU**   103
Josh Webb

Chapter 7—**Final Days**   120
Rodey Webb

Epilogue: Hero's Farewell   132
Rodey Webb

*"One must savor life but not fear death
and view the two as part of the same process,
always looking through the eyes of wonder, beauty and awe."*

Josh Webb

Prologue

A live I Cried is a collection of short stories depicting my son's battle against leukemia and how our family coped with his illness. Writing was his passion. This book is his inspiration. He chronicled the events of each day and documented the trials he faced. Words were his release, his way to purge the fear and elude unwelcome thoughts. I am merely his agent—a catalyst in accomplishing a dream and fulfilling a dying request.

After his diagnosis of AML (acute myelogenous leukemia) on February 14, 1994 my son endured unbearable pain and suffering, but none as great as during his final days. Josh fought a valiant fight, losing the battle only three months after his twenty-ninth birthday.

Josh followed all the procedures recommended by the medical establishment including traditional chemotherapy, bone marrow transplantation and T-cell infusion, and tried every other modality available—from holistic and macrobiotic remedies to vitamin supplements and a diet filled with cancer-fighting nutrients. He continually searched for innovative technology and new information. The doctors did not expect him to survive in 1994 or 1995 or 1996 or 1997; he continued to baffle the medical community with his amazing recoveries. Josh was a pioneer. His relentless search for a cure led him from Massachusetts to California. His insistence on trying even the most obscure treatments sparked physicians to create unusual combinations of manufactured drugs and native elements; but ultimately he would succumb to a disease too powerful even for his unflappable strength. The final round of chemotherapy, his last chance of restored health, damaged his heart and lungs and aged his body, reducing his stride to the shuffle of a ninety-nine-year-old man. Josh had titanic strength of mind and a fierce determination to conquer his disease. He fought so hard, so courageously, but the leukemia won.

Throughout the various stages of their lives, I wished for so many things for my children ... good friends, successful careers, happy marriages and, selfishly, grandchildren. In retrospect, these seem trivial. At this junction in life, I wanted one thing only—a healthy son. I wanted him free from the daily terror, free from the shadow of death. I wanted him back on the river paddling his canoe, back on his skis trekking through the snow, back writing the tales he loved to weave. It's not the natural rite of passage for parents to bury their children. My children were supposed to cry at my funeral.

Josh canoeing on the Chenango River

Josh was a multifaceted individual with a variety of interests. He was the proverbial outdoorsman and taught me to enjoy the wonder and beauty of nature with her symphonic sounds, her majestic peaks and her vibrant colors. With his gregarious personality, he was an inspiration to family, friends and the entire community, whether leading the Boy Scouts on camping expeditions, coaching the Odyssey of the

Mind® or teaching handcrafting skills to his crew. Josh valued his friends, no matter their age, nationality or background.

He was a contradiction of character, a philosopher, deep and introspective, yet one who loved the simple humor of Homer and Bart Simpson. I can still hear him laughing at Homer's idiotic antics as we watched together day after day. His music, too, was diverse, ranging from Brahms and Beethoven to the Doors and Pink Floyd. He was forever exploring new horizons, whether challenging the white water rapids of the Colorado River, climbing the picturesque peaks of the Adirondacks or skydiving and watching the blue skies tumble around him.

But what he loved most was writing short stories and poetic verse. He longed to be a published author. His ultimate dream was to write a screenplay re-capturing the bravery of Admiral Byrd and his crew as they explored the frozen tundra of the North Pole. He wanted to portray the strength of the human spirit when faced with insurmountable odds.

When he conceived the idea for *Alive I Cried*, he asked me to pen a chapter relating my parental views. I was surprised. I am not a writer. I possess no literary skills. He, however, was a philosophy and journalism major in college and had been honing his talent for years, freelancing for the local newspapers. He was confident we would write a best seller.

His death is a tragedy—a young man struck down in the prime of his life. Completing his book was extremely difficult yet somehow therapeutic. It surprises me what flows from within. It's a cleansing process as demons are faced. As I document his ordeal, a compelling and complex man emerges. Did I really know this man who wrote so eloquently? He was not a saint. He had his faults. Yet did I really know the man he grew to be, a man I'm proud to call son?

I believe all things happen for a reason, defying logic and comprehension. I believe my son's death brought the medical community one step closer to conquering this dreaded disease. Valuable information was gleaned from yet another human guinea pig—a man who laughed when he wanted to cry, a man whose optimism never faltered, a man whose humor carried us through our bleakest days.

Josh loved life and lived it to the fullest. He created a light in our lives never to be extinguished and certainly never forgotten. His literary gift, his appreciation of life and his love of mankind were meant to be shared, alive forever in written form.

For four, torturous years the entire family fought the disease together. Josh never fought alone. Burying our son is the most difficult thing we will ever do. Our nightmare is ended; our heartache remains.

I hope people from every walk of life will gain strength from his inspiring words and summon the courage to persevere through life's adversities.

Author's Note: *The content of Chapters One, Two, Five and Six was written by Josh Webb and remains unedited and in its original form.*

Josh's unfinished Chapter 6 (ICU) was written in 1997 in the latter stages of his disease. His concentration was diminished, but he was still driven to write and to impart his zest for life.

∞

... Beginnings

Trapped in the tangled web of daily existence, my life is harried, my pace often frenzied. I am heedless of my surroundings. I've become too busy to enjoy life's simple pleasures ... walking the beach, reading a book, or dining with friends. I've tossed aside my childhood dreams; I've overlooked the fact life can change in a split second and leave me unprepared; I've failed to remember true wealth lies in a loving family, faithful friends and good health. A mistake I will never make again.

In 1986, after twenty years of marriage, I faced what I thought would be the most difficult time of my life—making the arduous decision to end my marriage. At the ages of thirteen and seventeen, my children were extremely vulnerable and my actions created continual turmoil in their young lives. Little did I know the most stressful time still lay ahead.

The Webb family, 1985

Then, in 1989, when my daughter graduated from high school and my ex-husband's engagement eliminated all hope of reviving my marriage, I realized it was time to physically move on, to eliminate the bittersweet reminders of my former life and everything I had treasured—

my husband, my home and my friends. Living in a small town had become excruciatingly painful.

In January, 1990 (with the Christmas holiday and my children's departure for their respective colleges behind me) I made arrangements with the moving company, packed the car and bid my friends farewell. With the car loaded and tears flowing, I moved six hundred miles south to a new life in a strange city. An already tumultuous situation further escalated in November, 1990 when their father remarried, acquiring a new wife with a ready made family of five. It was a traumatic time for everyone.

My children were angry with me for disrupting their lives. The divorce caught them unawares, embroiling them in an emotional tug-of-war. The refuge of home and hearth evaporated, creating feelings of abandonment and loss. Their security was gone.

In their minds, I was escaping. It was impossible for them to understand all the memories and bonds created during twenty years of marriage—memories I can never forget. There is no escape.

However great these past upheavals, they were incomparable to the devastating phone call I received at five o'clock the morning of Valentine's Day, 1994 from the emergency room of a small county hospital. My son had been visiting his girlfriend at college and was rushed to the hospital in incredible pain. *Diagnosis:* Leukemia! In an instant our lives changed forever.

As the rural hospital was ill-equipped to treat the magnitude of the disease, he was transferred to a state-of-the-art facility in Albany, New York. My trip north still remains a blur. Directed to the fourth floor cancer unit by a volunteer at the information desk, I frantically searched for my son. I was on the verge of panic, when Doreene, a petite, brown-eyed nurse approached me and began to relate his medical condition just as Julie arrived with her father and stepmother.

Nurse Doreene and Josh, 1994

Rarely communicating with my ex-husband in the years following the divorce, I wondered how the scenario would unfold. Awkward at first, we established new parameters, setting aside previous animosity. We stood as one unit, a broken family united against a terrible disease. With conflicting emotions of terror and optimism, we would watch our son over the next four years wage a valiant battle.

Josh loved to write, particularly short stories and poetry. He began spinning his imaginative tales while still in grade school, illustrating them in pencil and crayon. (I still have those treasured drawings.) While a student at St. Lawrence University, two of his short stories were published. And following graduation, he freelanced for local newspapers before joining the family business.

Throughout his adult life and his many adventures, he continued to keep a journal. Even after he became ill and often too weak to speak, he was compelled to write. Not only did it serve as a way to purge himself of unwanted horrors, it also served as a way to communicate his passion for life. Thus began the birth of *Alive I Cried;* however, death forced his dream to become mine.

This is a remarkable book. Written from very different, very personal perspectives, each chapter uncovers an unique level of passion. The patient agonizes as mortality is faced; a fraternity brother mourns the loss of youth before its time; a fiancée grieves for a love unfulfilled and a younger sister, struggling for recognition, reveals her conflict and turmoil. Palpable throughout the book is the inconsolable heartache of a mother, powerless as she watches her son struggle to survive.

"Sermons To Myself" unfolds as Josh is driven to the hospital for a bone marrow transplant, an often fatal, month-long internment. His story is a celebration of life's joys as seen through the window of superlative horrors. It examines science as savior and explores the expanse of human emotion as a source of beauty and healing.

"From Bed to Bedside" examines the emotional upheaval shifting from the patient, following his successful bone marrow transplant, to loving grandson holding vigil at his grandfather's deathbed.

The bonds of fraternity life are depicted in **"Relapse."** Written in the voice of a fraternity brother, Josh writes of the fear a brother faces as he watches his young friend's life fade, and of the guilt impossible to keep at bay. Gone are the carefree days of college when the brotherhood was formed and dying was inconceivable.

Written by Josh, **"The ICU"** is an incomplete chapter. Through the eyes of his fiancée, Josh writes of her helplessness as she watches him lie near death for eight hellish days in the *Intensive Care Unit.*

As the final book revisions were made, I browsed through Josh's journals checking for inadvertent discrepancies and found a poem he had written in December, 1996. It revealed the immense depth of his fear, dramatically documented in poetic form. His tremendous distress shattered my broken heart. My fears were always hidden beneath the surface of smiles and optimism.

Uncertainty
by Josh Webb

My tortures overtake me
My mind swirling, sinking
Contaminated with the conditioning of relapse
Waiting, waiting ... the fearful, nervous anticipation
Of the whack to the back of my head
It always comes
The swollen glands, the sore throat
The infinitesimal weakening
"Is that it? Is it here? Has it returned to tear me apart?"
My mind a dark house and alone like a scared old woman
Defenseless
Paranoia, listening for noises, signs
Or in my fear do I open the door for its return?
It turns myself against myself
Disassembly, fragmented parts
Trying to pull together pieces as I cry on my knees on the floor
My only cure is crying
Exposure ... before God
This is me, this is my life
Crucified
And we must learn to love our fate
And now, breathing, I am thankful
Visions clear and clean, a pulsing kaleidoscope
Dance, love, sheen
Am I just greedy to want more?
It is the thirst of a young man
His yearning
For a canvass on which to paint his dreams
And with motherly assurances
I will be fine, I will be fine.

Throughout his illness I was right where I wanted to be, by his side. It gave me comfort. It gave him hope. Finding this poem confirmed the necessity of those motherly assurances, no matter how useless or powerless I felt.

Conflicting feelings surface as our incredible four-year struggle is relived in published form. My gratification in accomplishing Josh's dream, however, far outweighs any reservations I may have had. My son felt his insight and optimism could inspire others to persevere. He believed in the strength of the mind, believed in himself despite the odds. Recovery was possible! His first story, "Sermon's to Myself," was submitted to the various publishing houses but received only notices of rejection. How elated he would have been to see his writings published! Seven years after his death, the dream is realized, his dying wish fulfilled.

Mother and son, 1995

∞

1
Sermons to Myself

I am facing the very real prospect of my death and I am beginning to know God ... becoming aware of certainties within myself. I am examining faith. When the mind of man is in awe of that which he depends on for life, the ripe berries, the animals he hunts, and their incomprehensible origins, functions, beauty ... then there is the creation of God. I am in awe as I drive over this pre-dawn highway, under golden glowing lights, through miles of tunnels that burrow beneath impossible loads of earth, over bridges that span, to my limited mind, the unbridgeable. I am awake with thought. We learn more quickly under conditions of fear. This can reduce a man to the abject servitude of his torment or recast him in a mold made by a design of his own volition. The sun will soon rise and the prophets of medicine will begin the process of transplanting my bone marrow. This treatment might kill me, but without it, the leukemia likely will. Radiation and chemotherapy are effectively beyond my understanding, but they will lend to my salvation.

In a few hours I will be locked in a sterile room for a month in one of the best cancer institutions in the world. I am aided by Woden and Zeus. I have had three cycles of chemotherapy before, over the course of six months, to put me in some semblance of remission. I know the unrelenting bodily reduction of the modern cure, as ferocious and uncompassionate as the disease with which it grapples. I know the motionless writhing of warring titans battling for the spoils that are my life. I have had my immune system annihilated, have been the defenseless fodder of once innocuous bacteria and viruses. I have lived delicate, uncertain weeks with blood that would not clot, where a sneeze could cause an instant death. I know autonomy devoured, the paradise of my independence lost. I have had to rely on foreign hands to be bathed, fed and wiped. The transplant will be much the same, probably a bit worse. The sages, in their holy white gowns, described nearly having to kill me in order to save my life ... at best, an unwanted glimpse on the threshold of existence ... at worst, my death ... an elaborate, sadistic, incremental entombment. The people I love will have to wear gowns and masks and will be able to touch me only with gloved hands. I am a man alone crouching in the woods wrapped tightly in my own arms with head bowed to chest, weeping, and I am a man poised firmly and defiantly in a wind-blown field, arms raised and eyes ablaze. The greater my fear, the greater my strength.

I don't know what to make of this God of Science. He seems to be a god of two faces. He may have given me my disease in the first place, by creating the chemical fumes that I daily inhaled at the factory, and now he claims that I can be resurrected with his modern medicine. I am torn by a tempest cast by his hand, grateful beyond expression for this chance at another life, yet I remain suspicious and void of comfort. I stand before the chasm that separates rationality from reverence. The God of Science cleaved the world when he banished the old gods from the pantheon. He seized an unmappable empire and disregarded the needs of his people under the guise of granting freedom, yet this freedom is that of the orphan, fettered by emptiness. Science offers no solace for the trauma of living. With a yearning rekindled by fear, I have searched many ruins. I have read mythic tales, seen archetypal visions. My spirit is free, and many gods walk by my side. The sun is now beginning to rise, coloring the sky over the horizon in deep red, and I am awed by the beauty of Aurora. It is a vision of the coming of my new blood from the heavens.

My body has been graphed in preparation for the procedure. I have been mapped and delineated. A series of tattoos precisely marks the location of certain glands that need to be virtually obliterated. I feel like DaVinci's Sketch, an anatomical Everyman, holy as I stand with limbs outstretched within the circle, drawn in a time when science was intertwined with art and laced with humble reverence. The prophets will align my tattoos under the cross-hairs of the radiation machine and then blast me with a sub-atomic wind, a nuclear maelstrom, invisible to my senses. For my body it will seem like the apocalypse, cellular screams and convulsions, disorienting fury of fever; it is a tactic of last resort. Perhaps someday when the God of Science is more advanced, a future race of people will view this procedure as savage, a desperate tribal torture, but it is the cleansing ritual of our age. I abandon myself to the wisdom of my people with anxious fears and hopes.

There are certain oracles who claim that healing comes as an act of will, that impassioned expressions have a healthy physiological response. I believe this. I am also my own salvation. I have faith that my convalescence can be enhanced by the revelation of emotion ... the gateway to self-knowledge ... wave-laden reservoirs, in hidden caverns, of timeless human tales. Reason has no place here. There are messages of mythic realities etched in the sunken sands of a collective, yet individual Atlantis. Emotional discovery is the archeological exhumation of a civilization suspended in disaster. It is the release of a kaleidoscope of passion. The intuitive awareness of self and spirit, of religion and reality, roll and blend with fluid grace like liquid elements of an elixir that purges disease. I have learned to let free every emotion, from those that come in whispers to those that come in howls. With ancient awakening, I love, with deliberate upheaval, I cry. Every feeling that is revealed, a panacea; every one left buried, a poison. All of my expressions, no matter how painful, are a glimpse at the monument of my own humanity, a sip from the cistern of my soul. I feel; therefore, I am.

In my experience of these newfound, superlative pains and joys, my capacity for empathy is magnified. As one can feel vibrations, the underlying resonance of musical instruments, I feel the emotions of others. I am shaken by grand orchestrations both delightful and haunting—the ethereal overture of the birth of a child, the sweet serenade of lovers held in fond embrace, the operatic wail of a handicapped man struggling to walk, the cacophonous, riveting cantata of a soul in mourning. I listen to the music of the world everyday. There are quiet, melodious rhythms that accompany diminutive, nearly hidden pleasures ... the silent sonata of a conversation amongst friends ... the unsung duet of a mother walking hand-in-hand with her child. There is harmony in the daily joys I secretly witness. I am healed by sights and sounds.

I am passing by a high-rise building, an unnatural protrusion of glass and steel, glittering with lights, an aesthetic temptation of spangled promise. It dwarfs the steepled church by its side and outshines the stained glass. Because of my velocity, it feels as though I am sucked into the massive tunnel that the highway enters, quickly twisting and turning, and I feel shifting pressures, accentuating the catharsis of movement. I am a sponge being wrung. I rise from the subterranean labyrinth on an incline of asphalt and am thrown into the center of Metropolis, struggling to gain my bearings like a captured warrior suddenly tossed into the coliseum. I am surrounded by the towering idols of finance and industry. Off-ramps coil and slip between buildings, racing cars give rise to a hiss as the highway winds for miles above the city ... it is serpentine.

My faith is in medicine, blind for lack of understanding, hopeful in the light of its preachings. My faith is in myself, gaining clarity as I crystallize, the empowerment of self-awareness. I am redefined as I look upon my vision in the mirror, with loose patches of hair clinging to my otherwise bald head—dark, sunken, holocaust eyes. I am standing in a thin, sad reminder of my former physical self. Yet here I find my deepest dignity, and as I see my tightened skin sharply defining my rib cage, I also see my endurance, and as I witness the concavity of my abdomen I am reminded of my hunger to live. As I view my legs trembling under the pressure of my own weight, I know the vast extent of my strength. I do not conceal or augment my haggard visage, this outward expression of my inner conflict. I attract stares. Children cower behind the legs of their parents upon my approach, as though I were a wicked product of science fiction. When I animate with laughter or well-up with excitement, however, I am seen in a different role. I am mythical meek. As I walk and breathe, I am David fighting Goliath. People are in awe as they witness my experience of daily joys, as if my child-like smiles were stones thrown at the head of my enemy.

I know that in life there is a first breath and a last. There is the awakening induction into existence as the air of the world, fragranted with all that it touches, passes through lips wetted with amniotic fluid, expanding lungs fresh from the womb of creation ... vaporous nectar wantingly inhaled ... it is a sacred celebration of primordial baptism. There is also a dying breath ... an actual, final, irrevocable escape of air, with which we voice our last farewell ... sorrow-laden symbol of eternal parting from all that we have come to know and love. Between the first and the last are millions of other beautiful breaths, eloquent exchanges of air like the rhythmic sway of a conductor's wand, and yet they are scarcely noticed until we begin to lose them. I know the horrific, primitive panic of suffocation, as an unexplainable hemorrhage filled my lung with fluid. I know the salty, metallic taste and the viscous gasping like a criminal choking me in a pool of my own blood. During the day-long struggles with draining tubes and through the fitful nights of gurgling and panting, I wept for the years that I had spent unaware of the beauty of breathing, the joy of a sigh, the graceful swirls of an exhale on a cold winter's day.

It seems that we never appreciate the view from the mountain until we have fallen into the valley and then struggled to regain our former ground. Breathing is reverence with an empirical anchoring. This natural, basic joy is sacrosanct. Monks sit in the lotus position and breathe in through the nose and out through the mouth for spiritual grounding ... it is a consecrated symbiosis, breathing the breath of goddess earth, as in a kiss. To inhale is to be aware of the bellows' blow that fuels the fire in the heart, and to exhale is to be aware of the eddy-currents that are stirred as we waft on our limited passage through time. With unblocked lungs and an unclouded mind I release thankful hosannas into the air I breathe.

I have prepared myself for the chemotherapy that will be cleansing my veins and the radiation that will be sweeping my body. I welcome the scientific sacraments of exorcism. I seek peace with that which I do not understand, and the deepest harmony with that which I do. Weeks of meditation have buttressed my being. Winds of thought and winds of fear have eroded all that is frivolous and unnecessary, the fabricated images, material cravings, the harbored animosities, and have left exposed that which is irreducible ... my love, my joy, and my will ... the foundational fire of the heart, escalated to conflagration by the removal of a smothering fringe. I burn of a timeless and immortal source of the first human fire.

My scientific treatments have already prolonged my life, although in the context of my extended, excessive agonies, they may be merely prolonging my death. Perhaps they have granted me the time to save myself. When turmoil and terror are confronted, admitted, they become a means of transformation. Disease attacks an old self and not a new. When terror is denied, it becomes an ally of cancer, furthering self-destruction. I know that I stand in a firing line with my comrades on the ward, with no blindfold, and that the odds have it that certain of us will fall ... some during first treatment, some from failing to make it into remission, others during bone marrow transplants. There is death all along the roadway and it is putrid. Ed and I frequently discussed our hopes of healing while we played cards, he had the room next door. Same age, same disease ... scared soldiers caught in a war we didn't want, bonded by shared agonies. He had one of those contagious laughs, wildly uproaring, one that made me smile even when I heard it through the wall, especially when I knew that he was toying with the nurses. When he died, I shook my head from side to side frantically, unconsciously, as I did daily, hourly, in my bed, shaking the vomit from my mouth, expelling the bitterness, the rancid reality.

Watching my blood brothers and sisters die is watching my own death. I have seen their sheet-covered, lifeless bodies wheeled by the window of my room. This is the most penetrating fear that I have ever known. I have to constantly remind myself of my uniqueness ... a tenet of my personal religion, an attempted step away from my proximity to my fallen friends. There will undoubtedly be people on the bone marrow ward that will die. It is an unbending law. In my search for strength I preach that there are denominators, personal practices that increase my odds. I am constantly the focus of my thoughts. I search for elevation as the flood waters rumble. The secret to my health is the secret to my happiness.

I want to see the beauty that is always before my eyes. There is a stream that I venture to, where I can be alone. I sit upon a lush carpet of soft moss, pious in nature's pew, and listen to the flowing water as it dances toward the sea. I am of the same congregation as the deer and daffodils, singing in a jubilant chorus with crickets and chickadees. I savor being surrounded by the brown furrowed trunks of trees as they rise to glorious heights into spreading canopies and mystical spires. I obey the blue jay as he sounds the call to prayer from evergreen minarets. I inhale the sweet scents of the forest deeply and then return the air to the wind. I hear the drumbeat of my heart and the chiming of the cascading water. I am aware of synchronization, of uncarved beauty, both in myself and in the world; there is alignment, connection, and I tingle as though there were fireflies under my skin.

As I explore myself I explore my gifts. I preach sharing them. This is the conscious recognition of my humanly worth. We all give birth to fruits on the trees of our lives, talents and traits mighty and small. Quantity is not important, provided that what we cultivate is available for the nourishment of others. This is the sustenance that fulfills our social needs. It is a beautiful cycle of sowing and reaping. I am a storyteller, my friends enjoy listening, and with animation and vibrance I breathe new life into common tales of the past, of childhood scheming, of foibles and glories. I fabricate hopeful visions of the future. Then I listen. I am held by the hands and lore of others. As we are with one another there are joviality and love, there is catharsis in the sharing of pain, there is bond ... we are somehow, mysteriously in these moments, interwoven, and again I feel tingling, as though a magical medicine were released into my blood.

I asked my doctor about this tingling in my skin, which also travels down my spine, for it is relatively new to me, mainly since my treatments began. I have had the experience before, when feeling a particularly gripping poignancy, but now it occurs with much greater frequency, several times per day. He said that he had never heard of a patient experiencing any such phenomena, and he asked if I wanted to take something that might get rid of it. I explained that it was pleasant, and that surely at some point in his life, during moments of extreme emotion, he must have felt a similar physiological response. He looked at me in disbelief, probing me with sharp eyes of scrutiny, as though he thought my mental health was buckling under the pressure of my disease. It was as if I had asked him if he had ever seen a vision of the Virgin Mary.

I believe in the internalization of scripture, regardless of source ... conscious steps on a pathway to the soul. The border between metaphor and reality becomes less distinct as the gravity of my situation is intensified. I am Lazarus, being reborn, I am the Buddha, attaining enlightenment through meditation, I am Lao-tzu, seeking truth as water seeks the valley. I am leading myself to the fragrant gardens of peace of mind, an oasis of impunity in the valley of the shadow of death. I have walked through deserts of discontent in hospital halls, I have felt horror's breath on the back of my neck as I gazed into vanquished eyes ... at a gowned waif awaiting death, a would-be woman, too young to know independence, caught in a vortex of adolescent uncertainty, her soul outpouring a tempest of tears, yet her eyes shedding none. In a strangled, vacant whisper she uttered, "I guess the only thing that can save me now is Jesus," as if expecting deliverance by corporeal arms with wounded wrists, and I wanted to grasp and shake her into the realization of the Jesus within herself. I could never coax her out of bed to walk with me, just for a little exercise, to get the blood moving. Now her blood is silent and still ... indelible vision before my eyes. My sense of horror and misery have been redefined as a character in this grave drama ... life's lessons amplified as my attention remains wholly focused. I've seen people transformed by the testaments, entranced by the rosary and hypnotized by the cross ... they fare well against disease.

I have learned from children. A child's world is filled with gods ... walking, breathing, smiling gods ... parents, teachers, doctors ... so that when children are stricken with cancer, the likelihood of their recovery is very great, much better than an adult with an identical affliction. The spiritual seed of youth, possessing just the beginnings of stem and root, is easily nourished by the caring sustenance of elders, who are viewed in a holy light as the omnipotent caretakers of all wisdom. When a child is daily informed by a host of gods that he will rejuvenate, the boogie-men of doubt are purged, confidence is instilled, creating a luxuriant greenhouse conducive to good-healing. Further assurance is given through a barrage of affection, a touch of the divine. Children are inclined to display their feelings. Their tender faces of innocence are the windows of their emotion. If children are afraid, they are not compelled to hide it, they are not clouded by the shoulds and oughts of proper social conduct. When relieved of their fear, they can get on with the playful business of their lives, running in the tall grass and rolling with laughter in piles of leaves ... in this too there is healing. Many religions recognize that a successful life is approached with the heart of a child.

I think I am superstitious. I eat a head of broccoli every day and drink a pint of carrot juice for the anti-carcinogens. Fruits and vegetables are my daily communion. There are schisms of the medical community that exult the healthy diet as a means of purifying the body. Their evidence is limited and beyond my understanding, less documented than the scriptures of the high priests of hematology, who largely ignore these separatists, but I abide by their wisdom. I equate, perhaps without reason, that which is natural with that which is healthy, and hence I have faith in my habits. I feel reverent as I eat my fruits, savoring the succulence, thankful for the life which in turn provides me with life.

The fears that I normally have when I'm driving on the highway are now absent, my everyday concerns dissolved. My car will not break down, I will not get a flat tire. I suspect that my confidence is irrational, but this is the nature of faith. Last year my friend, in this same city, on the same highway, became lost and drove into a bad neighborhood. He left in an ambulance, with a knife in his chest. He suffered from a similar cancer, individuals forgetting what is sacred, caused by an unknown social dis-ease. Perhaps all evils are born of the same source. Statistically, I stand a much greater chance of surviving lost in the city's back alleys than I do on the bone marrow ward, but I am beyond probabilities and numbers, confident that my survival is dependent on far more than a roll of the technological dice.

When the mind of man is terrified by inexplicable and overpowering forces, the raging floods, cataclysmic earthquakes, and their incomprehensible origins, powers, destructions ... then there is the creation of God. Man wonders what he has done wrong, or if he is simply subject to the mercy of a capricious and spiteful deity, whose world is incongruous, the nonsensical amalgamation of good and evil. The God of Science is both Lucifer and Jehovah, newborn, alone, and wrenched by the splitting neurosis of His contradictory duality. He feeds the newfound masses of the world with His methods, and then gives them cancer with pesticides ... houses millions in towering cities that devour themselves with crime, tries to bring world peace with computerized bombs. He must scream thunder from the ruins of Olympus.

I sometimes wonder what I have done wrong. Of what sinful fruits did I partake that cast me, decrepit and alone, from the garden of good health? What serpent whispered in my ear? The prophets are concerned only with cure, not cause, and so, at times, I entertain my own metaphorical legend of my personal fall. I was partly led astray by the seductive promise of devilish cherubs, apparitions of a commercial reality, lending me aspirations. Discontentment is disease. I worshipped a false idol ... religion is always a way of life. I chose to work for fifty hours every week in the chemical air of cinder block catacombs, feeding on the droppings from vending machines, licking the grease from the fast-food machinery. I never saw the holiness of my body or that happiness is a venerated state of mind. I scurried about collecting the material items of my security, as if satisfaction could be hand-held.

There is no certain cause of my illness. It may have been scripted into my genes from the day of my conception, a pre-timed destruction that at any other epoch in history would have been unalterable. Fabricating external sources for the direction of blame will not aid in my convalescence when my cancer is embedded within myself. There is no reward in cursing against that which has already taken place, as if the grim dealings of fate could be swayed by rhetoric illustrating their injustice. It is best to make peace with the past, in the faith that events happen for reasons, while never forgetting that certain aspects of one's future can be controlled, at least influenced, by a tenacious will, an intimacy with one's feelings ... a rapport with the gods.

People pray for me, and I am moved to my foundations ... their concern welling-up so forcibly that it reaches the heavens. Their letters, as they inundate my room, their sympathies, as they diffuse through the contact of our hands, their prayers, as they race through the ether, are all divine interventions, and I am healed, cleansed, an ablution with holy water distilled of human kindness. Children have sent me drawings whose radiance makes me weep ... crayon masterpieces emanating the purity and refined beauty of youthful hope and joy, overflowing with the exuberant encouragement of innocent minds ... pictures of me crushing the villain of cancer, arms raised in triumph, or laughing as I bravely plunge over the waterfall of my turbulent treatments ... these are cornucopias of the sweetest delights, artwork worthy of any museum display, and as I bear witness to them I am reminded of all that is good in the world, filling me further with the desire to remain alive, keenly alive ... so that I too may give gifts immeasurably grand.

I see the world as three webs of life. In the first, I am the web itself, intricate, wondrous, composed of myriad gossamer spokes emanating from a common convergence, iridescent and illuminated, a burst of brilliance, myself, whole. Some of the strands in the web of myself represent my elements of character, my strengths and passions, my fears and weaknesses. I have been marred by the weather, torn and tattered, yet am resilient and immune. I have been woven by the lifetime history of my trials and triumphs ... a displayed celebration of all that I have learned. I am the tender filaments that are my body, my veins and tendons, the malleable muscles of my face, the delicate arrangement of my hands as I dexterously flex and grasp. I am the mysterious molecular complexity of my flesh and blood and, like all webs, I will not last forever. I am a sorrowfully evanescent creation of wonder in the vast pastures of time.

In the second web, I am merely the center, and the spokes that radiate outward represent my friends and family, townsfolk bringing good cheer ... the sum of my human connections, all whom I have ever touched. The threads that hold us together seem tenuous, invisible to the hurried passer-by, but are remarkable in their strength as they withstand wind and gale, holding the web as one. This is the sweet adhesion that embraces the human race. The individual fibers of emotion that constitute this glorious web are nearly imperceptible, but when the breadth of their beauty is fully realized, fully felt, it is as if the web glistens with beaded jewels of dew, brilliant in the morning sun, beaming with shimmering clarity the spectrum of emotion ... prisms of love and laughter, rays of tears and woes.

The third web is the universe, and I am a small point on its fringe, barely visible, yet connected to all things. I am of the same substance and pattern that gives rise to the cosmic waltz of the planets, the majestic symphony of wolfsong, the endless howl of the sweeping wind. I am of the silken threads that are the veins of civilization, language and legends, tribes and empires. I drink of the circuitous flow that is the mist, the rain, and the river. My flesh is of the earth. My cells are filled with the salt of an ancient ocean. My mind is the treasured inheritance of that which is logic and that which is myth. I am connected to the primeval expressive impulses that are cave paintings and jungle statues long since overgrown. I am the wanting flower nestled beneath the forest floor, craving the slightest trickle of the sunlight that also churns the air and the seas. I possess the perpetual hunger that fuels the savage, glorious drama of life and death. I partake of the timeless divinity that laces the world. My voice is part of the wailing chorus that implores the heavens.

I have arrived. The sun has risen and I can see the hospital, temple of healing. I wanted to bring myself here alone, symbol of independence, to collect my thoughts, to deliver these sermons to myself.

My beloved family will be here shortly, source of an infinite, ancient security, from whom transfuses the inexplicable essence of life itself ... and from my sister, a grail full of marrow, holiest of gifts. I marvel at the glory of my family tree, and I, a wounded limb, am caught by outstretched arms and am grafted back to the trunk anew. My flesh and soul resonate. I am prepared for what I must undergo. I am aflame with the ungrounded and timeless desire to stay alive, and, in my knowledge of all that is within me and all that surrounds me, I have faith that I will live. I am mortal, born of the earth. I am spirit, born of the ether, my own god.

$$\infty$$

2 From Bed to Bedside

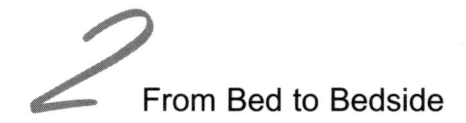

You try to retain your sanity by thinking about forested hills and pastures. Last night your one hundred and five degree fever made you dream that you were being burnt at the stake, you felt your skin blister and char, and now you are trying to pull yourself together by concentrating on familiar sylvan settings. A stream trickles down worn stone. The other night doctors in black gowns tried to get you to sign your own death certificate. Dew covers a blade of grass; wildflowers bow toward the sun. Whether in dream or meditation, you always end up back in your hospital bed. Your reality is a series of nightmares. You have not eaten a fragment of food or sipped a spoonful of broth since you vomited the lining of your esophagus in tubular, choking segments and, like the cancer that was in you, your body is feeding upon itself to stay alive. You are living a holocaust existence. Hands reach out of the clouds every four hours to check your vital signs. The caustic gnawing of chemotherapy has been like a premature decay for your body. Your musculature has become atrophied ... thin tissues connected to bone. You can barely roll over. The constant force of gravity pulls you further into your bed and you feel as though you are slowly melting into your mattress like a carcass slowly melting into the earth. You hang on by thinking of forested hills and pastures.

The doctors say that everything is going as planned. Your sister's marrow has colonized the hollow ruins of your bones and has begun to escalate your blood counts. You have survived the teetering vulnerability of the transplant's most serious weeks, yet are still like a premature baby kept in a state of well-monitored incubation. You have no natural defenses in your exposed sprawl of underdevelopment, and a sterile room provides sanctuary against bacteria and viruses. Antibiotics only give you a limited, *Fisher-Price* immune system. Your new umbilical cord is a line of plastic tubing that burrows into your chest, where nurses remove blood for testing and through which you are fed treatment ... it is a placental interface with your sexless medical parentage. It gets tangled around your neck and arms while you sleep. You constantly hear the murmuring of a mechanical pump that is responsible for initiating peristalsis in this dangling lifeline, filling you with the blood products of kind strangers.

In your temporary moments of lucidity, you marvel at your mother's unfaltering patience ... she has sat by your side for every waking second of these everlasting weeks, daily clad in gown, mask, and thick rubber gloves in the odd environment of this oversized incubator. She attends to the needs that medicine cannot provide you, conveying love in a glance even when your eyes are barely open to receive it. She provides an unconscious assurance of security in your most uncertain moments. You are aware that your disease, terrible as it has been, has brought you closer to her. She often covers you with blankets and gives you a motherly tucking-in. She is protective. Sensing medical fallibility, she asks to know every chemical they inject into you, every pill they want you to take, watching for allergies and inadvertent overdoses. You sleep most of the day. She nervously notes the finer changes in the pitch of your breathing ... the many unsettling hesitations and pauses.

Your father does not possess a waiting-room composure. He tries to be silently supportive, but the collision with his fundamental state of being is unmistakable, like an internal car accident. He desperately wants to alleviate your suffering, yet there is nothing he can do. He tries to be patient, yet he is unalterably kinetic. When he is not feeling the roar of helplessness, he is simply bored. There is little to talk about, you are usually too hazy for the happy distraction of conversation and there is never any new news ... your internment is just an extremely long, terrible wait. He taps his foot in discontent like a self-imposed water-torture. He often leaves the room in order to make phone calls or to take long contemplative walks down the streets of the city. Life-long reinforcements of good fortune have not prepared him for the shocking calamity of your ill-health. He believed that every problem had an easy answer until the contradiction of your tearful reality. His sole humble solution is to rub your back in slow, assuring sways ... his resignation to life's fated horrors, his voiceless expression of love.

Neither of your parents suspected they would see each other after their proprietous, muted meeting at your college graduation, at least not until your wedding day, and that would be the last of it. Your return to infancy echoes with unexpected reverberations of the past, a powerfully binding crib-trauma. You notice that they are getting along well; it has been good to see them hug again. There was something existentially disheartening about being exposed to the clash of your creators, a tacit, sorrowful banishment for the living symbol of dissolved union, as if marriage and children were just a bad idea. You recall some the ugly details of their tumultuous divorce and are now pleasantly surprised to witness the restoration of their rapport. You have no inner-child delusions that they will get back together, it is simply nice to hear them recounting the joyful remember-whens of their past. Their former dissonance has been replaced by a certain harmony. You always wondered how they could live, or possibly die, with such unaddressed anger, their last words to each other were nothing less than harsh accusations accentuated by the falling of a judge's gavel, a sad ending to half a lifetime together. Your illness has given them the time to reintroduce themselves to each other's forgotten virtues, and that, coupled with the fond recollections of happy times, has been enough for them to silently forgive one another, allowing them to be free of the burden of their animosity. You note that hospital rooms can bring about more than one type of healing.

It is time for you to walk, to begin reconditioning. You have permission to leave your sterile room. Your new blood cells have displayed sufficient vigor to grant you a limited functionality. In the event of an unexpected cut, you now possess enough platelets to halt the exodus of blood from your body, ample red cells to carry oxygen to your thirsting tissues, and enough white cells to put up a fight. Leaving your bed is the hard part. During the past month you have scarcely left your nest of blankets and pillows; there were only the precarious, leg-quaking weigh-ins, where two nurses kept you from falling off the scale, and the assisted transfers to the porta-commode where you felt as shapeless as your diarrhea. You have urinated exclusively while lying down, thanks to a convenient plastic container that others have shuttled to the toilet. You have lived a strange, ghastly existence upon a few square feet of mattress, around which friends have offered their sympathies and medical students have gathered to study, peering over one another's shoulders to gain a better look. Your bed has provided cushioned relief after the stress of lengthy, postured examinations ... it has been your haven and your prison, a kind refuge and a loathsome exile, and now it is time to leave it, if only for a few frightening, glorious moments.

You are sitting up, your mother forcing some undersized hospital booties onto your feet. You check all of your tubing, making sure that nothing will snag and rip the line out of your chest; your IV pole will be going with you. Your father is enthusiastic, finally bestowed with a tangible mark of progress, and he moves a chair out of the way so that the two of you can walk from the room abreast. You note that this is quite a production for what will inevitably be a very brief sojourn. Your mother helps you into another shirt that she thinks will insure your warmth, bending your arm back to get it into the sleeve.

"Just like the first day of school, chickenhead, here comes the bus," your sister cackles in laughter, poking fun at your mother's hyper-concern as well as the scattered population of loose hairs on your head. You appreciate her comic exploitations, bringing cathartic focus to the situation, knowing that it is healthier to admit than to ignore. She grabs a mock steering wheel and putters around the room, "Vroom, vroom ... chickenhead express ... going about ten feet and then returning." Her raw confidence in your recovery affords everyone the luxury of her humor. You look at her in feigned scorn because you don't have the energy to generate a decent verbal comeback. You tremble as your Dad helps you to your feet. Your sister breaks into an exaggerated tap dance routine immediately in front of you, "It takes one step and you're ready to go ... bump, bump ... two steps and you're off to the show ..." getting you back for all those superior report cards that you rubbed in her face.

You have literally never felt so weak in your life. You are profoundly debilitated, quivering as if you have just escaped the grave. Your first steps are tentative, a languid sequence of flat-footed scuffs and positionings, buttressed by the pillar that is your father, his arm around your back. He asks you if you're sure you want to go on, and you adamantly nod the affirmative. This degree of physical retardation is impossible to identify with, something one might see on an afternoon telethon, distinctly not you. You still have the will and self-image of the robust. Last summer you climbed Mt. Washington and Mt. Katadin within a couple of days and now you can barely shuffle across a polished floor. You pass through your doorway and enter the hall, a bit dizzy, your blood adjusting, no longer a stagnant pool. It takes a moment for your eyes to refocus in the brighter light.

"All right! Look who's out and about ..."

"Hey good lookin'!" "Nothing like a little exercise ..." come the charitable comments of your nurses as they lift their heads from the busyness of their duties ... they gather items from medical carts like bees darting between flowers ... a natural, bustling harmony. In defiance of your condition you establish the Herculean goal of walking thirty feet to a plate glass window before you will return to your room; you are in a different dimension, confined to boundaries that are beyond most people's imaginations. You progress in increments, your mother pushing the IV pole behind you, your sister egging you on, your father at your side, and after a short while you reach the window, bracing yourself against it with your arms, exhausted. You feel like you've been trampled. The pedestrian-march, ant-farm activity you witness in the world below is dumbfounding, you steam the glass with your breath and are so tired that you just want to get back to your room. You turn, your door appears to be on a distant horizon. Tears well in your eyes. An intern sees you struggling and suggests you take a wheelchair back. With vague and undirected anger you resolve to finish the marathon on your own accord. After a very arduous sequence of the same feeble steps, you finally make it back to your room and collapse in your bed, dizzy, face streaked with tears, yet silently elated.

* * *

In three and a half weeks you are walking alone with cautious steps down the sidewalk of your hometown, dressed neatly in clothes that are now exceedingly baggy. After your month-long hospitalization and the sedentary weeks of out-patient recovery, this little stroll seems like flight. You revel in your newfound independence. You were even able to tie your own shoes. You have seen this small town tens of thousands of times, but never with the eyes that you now possess, and it has never looked so beautiful. The glory is in the details, the radiance lies in hidden subtleties. You've never noticed the brilliant mosaic above the lintel of the church's side door, so fine in its patterned intricacy that it beckons to be admired. You see the always-ebullient Howard Jenkins take about nine blind steps forward while still turned backward in animated gestures of parting. The bell-tower clock is still reliably slow; the repetitious mechanical churning of the printing press tells you it's Thursday afternoon. The rain gutter of the grocery store drips from the bottom of a sag between joints, filled with yesterday's drizzle. This town is filled with old sights you feared you'd never see again and new ones that you never dreamed of. You see that Jane Hanson is out of her flowered maternity clothes and is carrying a beautiful baby. Crazy Daisy sits in her wheelchair across the street, so excited to see you that she stands up and waves as if you were a mile away. There is an ironically inviting allure in the dilapidated hovel they call a tavern, perched precariously on the river's edge. The soldier atop the civil war monument that guards the municipal park has a look on his stone face that is proud and resolute. This town sent you five or six hundred get-well cards, several flower arrangements, and at least a dozen batches of cookies. You walk into the park and lie down in the mowed grass with your arms and legs stretched out, gazing upward, something you have never done before; you cannot help but weep, for you know that you have made it back home.

Back in your apartment you are surrounded by the warmth of familiar, meaningful objects. You appreciatively draw your hand down the smooth top of the antique table that you and your mother spent several weekends looking for a few summers ago. On top of the table sit books that you recollect intimately, mixed with others that you've always intended to read but never got around to. The medical bag that your sister's bone marrow came in is pinned to the wall. Some things are still packed; you see the roll of posters that covered your bleak hospital walls, images of wolves and poets, of Jack London and vast landscapes, which said something about yourself when you were unable to. You ease yourself into your favorite cushioned chair and look into the photo album that your mother let you borrow, peering into it for the third time in as many days, starting with the pictures taken hours after your birth, a naked baby boy with a blue ribbon taped to his head, just as bald as you are now from the chemo. There's one of you walking gleefully in your one-piece pajamas, and another where you've fallen on the floor. There's a photo of you nearly strangling your terrified kitten with overzealous affection, and of smearing a fudgesickle all over the face of your newborn sister. You are frozen in time as a crazed little ham dancing wildly in a cowboy suit, the fringe of your jacket defying gravity. You show off your toad collection and peer out from your sofa cushion fort. You awkwardly dribble a basketball. You have a lot of acne in one photo with your parents and you don't look happy to be there. As you get older you fly off rope swings into rivers and ride snowmobiles. You merrily wax the hood of your first car. You look handsome at your prom. There's a picture of your father as a slimmer man with you on a mountain top, and another where you are embracing your first real love. One shot shows your devilish sister about to pour a bucket of water on your head as you unwittingly read by the lake. You are the happy scholar at your college graduation, in black cap and gown with your Mom in one picture, and with your Dad in the next. Then there are blank pages.

As you close the album you are inundated with a tide of emotion, head arced upwards as if looking for answers, knowing that the series of pictures you've just seen nearly served as the synopsis of your entire life, a finite display of images ending with a young man entering adulthood, punctuated by an obituary. Only now, after the experience, can you acknowledge that you were so close to death. Your mind races with images of those who died on your hospital hall, people like you who drifted slightly further into the horror and did not return. You imagine their photo albums, blank pages never to be filled ... smiling faces posed for the camera, happily unknowing one moment, a blissful flash of time, and then the sudden confusion of being bed-ridden with illness, the frightful wondering of where life has gone, recalling only highlighted fragments. You have felt the horror of deathbed forgetting, of trying to make sense of life in the panic of a few miserable days.

You know that your disease has altered you. You are not completely changed, but you have been accentuated. Before you were ill, you had vague notions of goodness, of joy and appreciation, but now your awareness has been cemented, indelibly etched in the slate of your mind. You have been tempered by suffering. You are thankful for every footstep, reverent with every breath. Your aesthetic has bloomed. You see beauty and significance as you pass from moment to moment. Your past is a colorful flowing whole, you have a future and it is gloriously thrilling, your present is keenly alive. Human contact, formerly unacknowledged or routine, is now a source of immeasurable delight, the living exchange of feeling from soul to soul. And though you were cursed with misery, you have been blessed with your family, with you in every moment, in your blood and in your mind, your father who would move the world for you if he only could, the absolute love of your mother, and the humorous affections of your only sister, all with you to any end.

As you are engaged in these pleasant thoughts of life, the phone rings. It is your father calling from his office on the other side of town. "I hate to have to tell you this, especially now, you've already been through enough for a lifetime," his tone is unusually melancholy, you are puzzled and your stomach sinks in anticipation of what he is about to convey. You wonder if he has talked to your doctors about your health. "The mayor was admitted to the hospital last night, it doesn't look good." His voice is tremorous. "Pick you up in fifteen minutes?" Shocked, you agree to go.

The mayor is your grandfather. In the car your father tells you that your grandfather has been diagnosed with a rare blood disease, which, like your leukemia, results from bone marrow gone bad. He has apparently had the disease for several years, but has not told a soul. Your family calls him mayor because unconsciously the title reveals the unspoken fact that the focus of his daily concerns lies more in municipal affairs than in familial devotion. It is often said with a sad tone of sarcasm. His love for his children and grandchildren is surmised but never spoken. He is an excellent mayor, he has held a record term, but his family's needs have not included the fixing of roads or attending to the municipal water supply. Your grandfather's marrow has stopped producing oxygen-carrying red cells, and without them the body suffocates on the cellular level and dies. You are not prepared for this. Your thoughts have centered around life's joys, around freedom and health, and this feels like a bad metaphysical joke. You feel an incredible mass of tangled emotion, for his faltering condition seems to be a mirror of your own, he could be dying, and beneath this superlative sorrow lies the disappointment wrought by years of his halfhearted interest in your affairs.

The antiseptic hospital air is thick with bad memories. You have just escaped this place and now fate is dragging you back in.

A sickly man draped in blankets is being wheeled into radiation therapy, you remember the way. You and your father walk down the hallway and find your grandfather's room. The door is open. Your heart rate increases. You peer in on the mountain of a man, lying in bed covered to the chest in white sheets. You note that this must have been what it was like to look in upon you. You try to harness your energy as you walk in. The scene is frightfully familiar. You note the IV pole with a blood pressure cuff draped over the pump box. You see the porta-commode next to his bed. It smells.

"Hi, Gramp!" you say, trying to rise above your known indignity of the setting.

"My God, look who's here. Boy, from what they were telling me I expected you'd look a lot worse," he says in a faint, meek tone that is contrary to your conditioned expectations. He hasn't seen you since the transplant. "You finally got a haircut," he kids of your baldness, trying to find his role, trying to establish a sense of normalcy.

"Well, Mayor, how do you like these deluxe accommodations?" your father asks, keeping above the pain of seeing his father in this condition.

"This isn't exactly the Super 8. Channel changer doesn't work and I can't see a goddamned thing out the window. Must have been a woman that designed that undersized plastic toilet, I sat down and crushed my testicles on the front of the seat," he complains in his typical Archie Bunkeresque manner. He puts all of his available energy into his demeanor, trying to create the appearance that nothing has changed. His face is pale from lack of cells. You can tell he's exhausted. He talks about the municipal duties he is neglecting by being infirm, taking refuge in his old standby, "If I don't get to work, I'll be impeached." This is foreign to him, he is not at ease. His own body has deprived him of his typical freedom. You help him take a drink of juice, holding the straw to his quivering lips. He labors to begin a conversation with your father about municipal decisions. You exit the room to get an update on his condition.

His doctor informs you that his blood counts are decreasing rapidly. Donor cells seem to be quickly devoured by his own antibodies, strangely recognizing the new cells as infecting invaders. The doctor shakes his head apologetically and says that your grandfather might have enough hemoglobin to get him through the week, but even that is optimistic. You feel like this is unreal, the content of bad dreams. It is too sudden. It is an injustice that makes you indignant, but there is nowhere to lash out, nowhere to pinpoint cause or blame. Your grandfather is slipping into the same dark pit that you were in and it doesn't look like he'll be coming out. He has to endure what you would never wish upon your worst enemy and, if you want to give him support, you have to watch. You've barely begun to recover from your own ordeal. You thank God that he's not taking any chemo or other treatment; he's an old man and it appears that it's time for him to go. For the last few months you've concentrated only on your own health, you've devoted no thoughts to final goodbyes. You are wrenched by the prospect of his absence, of the void, of the emptiness his death will create in your lineage. You hate to relive the horrors that you are trying to forget, yet there is no escaping it, people become diseased and die, this is what it is to be a participant in life.

You need time to think, to make peace with this reality. You struggle to climb three flights of stairs, pausing frequently to catch your breath. You know this hospital too well. It seems like a theater for your family's tragedies. You walk down the hall to your old room, approaching it cautiously, as if something inside could still hurt you. It is the lair of your most fearful demons. The room is unoccupied and you enter, peering at the dull blank walls. You were here for an entire month. It is haunting. Looking at the clock, you are transported back under the sheets, watching the second hand creep eternally. You remember clinging to a fragile sanity by meditating on forested hills and pastures. You see the pink plastic tub that caught the regurgitated pieces of your esophagus. You didn't think it would ever end. This place is just an empty generic cubicle. There is a plain bed with white sheets and a dime-store nightstand. It is stark and bleak. Yet here, as you suffered, you learned. You took the accelerated course in the values of life and you never had to leave the room. You realize that your grandfather will mercifully not have to suffer as badly as you did. He is an old man, without the fight. He has lived his life. Yet parting forever is not easy. You make your way back into the hallway, into the section of corridor where you had to learn to walk again, where you staggered and sobbed. You are aware that there is still time left for enjoyment and love, time to make the best of a terrible situation.

When you reenter your grandfather's room, he and your father are still talking. It is a pleasant scene. Not hearing their specific words, you drift off into the music of their intonations. In your grandfather's voice you can hear him telling the stories that shaped him, of depressions and wars, of him as a child crying for a meal and as a young laborer sweating in ditches for a dollar a day. He has always been a living window to the intimate, individual side of history. A constant progression of innumerable events, some vast and worldly, some diminutive and personal, have forged him and carried him into the present moment as he lies before you. You can sense his character, you can feel his charisma dimpled with colloquial flair. You understand why he is admired by an entire community. He is a jolly dynamo and always gets things done. You can see him flipping pancakes for benefit breakfasts and riding the floats in countless Fourth of July parades. You can also see the hard taskmaster and the cold stoic, the piercing reprimands and austere nonchalance. You remember your series of strivings that occasionally gained a pat on the back but more often went numbly ignored. Yet now you can forgive him. He has been molded by subtitles that are beyond your comprehension. His life has not been easy and he did the best he could. In that hospital bed, infirm, aware of his own impending demise, you wonder if he has any regrets.

The next day your aunt Hannah drives in from Maine, accompanied by her life-partner, a beautiful Asian woman named Suki. You wonder how well this will go. Your grandfather has not exactly approved of your aunt's lesbian lifestyle. It has been a perpetual thorn in his side. The last time Hannah brought Suki to a family gathering, your grandfather boycotted his own barbecue and the meat was left to blacken in the commotion like so many seared feelings. Hannah has deviated considerably from his conservative ideals. She hasn't made much money pursuing her "hokey" dreams as an organic farmer, living in a "potato crate" house on the edge of the woods. He has reasoned that she is doomed to fail because farming is husbandry and she doesn't have a husband. In spite of all of his condemnations, she is drawn here with the need to say goodbye. She moved away years ago in avoidance, the phone providing safe distance yet without embrace, hoping for a rapport that never fully came.

He is sleeping and your aunt walks quietly into his hospital room, followed by Suki. You and your sister and father are already beside him. The mood is black with sorrow and laced with nervous anticipation. He has gotten worse. He has slipped further. You watch the clammy skin of his chest rise and fall like a great bellows, stirring the air like the whir of the tides, his breath drifting in and out of the stagnant silence. You know where he is, you have been there. You have rested on that dark edge. Your father is drained, he has waited through these storms of illness for too long. Your sister lacks the luster of confidence that she had at your bedside and is uncharacteristically depressed. Your aunt approaches. She is wearing a medallion conspicuously around her neck, an award for women's achievement that she and her therapist agreed could be an amulet of strength in facing her ultimate symbol of male intimidation. She is thoughtful, mystical. She feels the need to touch him, and gently takes his limp hand. His heavy eyelids slowly raise and he takes a moment to make the transition from deep sleep to the conscious processing of the faces before him. He knows he is dying.

"My goodness," he says as he looks upon Hannah, speaking softly from fatigue, "My daughter." He hasn't seen her in over a year. He is glad she has come. He tightens his grip around her hand, augmenting his sensory awareness of her presence, making his experience of her more intense. He must have considered the loss that they each would have felt had she not made the trip, had there been no sense of closure or reconciliation. He looks upon her with delight and wonder, like he did on the day she was born, marveling at the woman now before him. In the depths where he was sleeping he abandoned his own aversions. He greets Suki warmly and offers embraces as though he wants to be touched by all. This is strangely beautiful. He comments that a curmudgeon like himself doesn't deserve such a fine gathering of people, and you hear the doubt within him, and you wonder if this is the first time or if he has suspected for years that he could have been more attentive to his family, that he could have been kinder, that the time could have been better spent. You know the pain of deathbed remorse, wishing you could go back and do it over again. He thoughtfully asks Hannah and Suki how they have been, what they have been doing, questions typical of reunion, which breed more questions, in his faint tone seeming to be genuinely concerned. Hannah's responses are filled with surprise and enthusiasm, the conditioned neglect of decades contradicted by an old man's sudden interest.

In the middle of conversation, your grandfather appears to be in a state of discomfort. His face grimaces in agony and he tries to move his body into a position that alleviates the pain, but he does not have the strength. You and your father help him to sit upright, to readjust, your hands having to find position on his soft awkward curvature. He complains of his lower extremities and you peer under the sheets to find his legs grossly swollen. Fluid is collecting in his extremities. There are purple blotches where his capillaries are bursting.

Suki sees him suffering. "I know some yoga exercises that might help you open up your energy," she says to your grandfather. "I teach a class to the oncology patients at our local hospital. Would you like to try?"

"Well," he hesitates. Yoga is an activity that would have always fallen into his "hokey" category, and from an Asian lesbian at that. "Do you think you can teach an old dog a new trick?"

"I'm sure of it," Suki says with a smile.

You wonder if he is politely appeasing or if he is acting from real desire. In either case, it is not typical. Soon Suki has your grandfather's arms moving in synchronization with his breathing and before long she has everyone in some form of stretch or contortion. It seems to make your grandfather feel better, and the foreignness of the activity lends itself to a warmly comic atmosphere. Your family is stuffed into a simple little room and no one has a single plan or commitment, you have the entire day to spend together. After the yoga fades, your sister proudly displays the scars left behind from the donation of her bone marrow, humorously situated at the top of her buttocks, nearly mooning the entire group and boldly exclaiming that she wants a new car for saving your life, your grandfather shaking the bed with his belly-laughter. Stories then abound. Your father tells tales of your grandfather's wheeling-and-dealing, of the time he sold an old truck for a side of beef, of his lead-foot and his roadside arguments with the law. You relate the incident when your grandfather met the mayor of New York City and said, "You think you've got problems. We've got a fire truck with a loose axle and our red light is on the fritz!" Your sister recalls her entire litter of kittens climbing up your grandfather's pant leg and refusing to come down, and then the ridiculous dance he had to do in order to get them out. He revels in hearing these old stories, reminding him of the times that he touched you all by virtue of his character. He looks so good and is having so much fun that you wonder if he might recover. Your Dad shares the tale where your grandfather accidentally felled a tree into Arnold Boorman's driveway, flattening the garbage can and then shouting, "You're lucky, Arnie, that could have easily been your house." In the laughter that accompanies the sharing of his past comedies and virtues, there is a type of healing occurring in spite of the vividness of his decline. These day-long recollections serve as a cathartic summary of his life, told while he is still alive, capable of happiness, making the best of a terrible situation.

In the middle of the fun, your grandfather has to go the bathroom, but he needs some help. Hannah assists with the aim and the holding of the urinal jug and you exclaim that when you're sick it doesn't matter who holds your phallus, recalling your loss of modesty in the midst of illness. Your aunt gazes down to check the progress, shouting, "My God, I've heard of these things but I've never seen one before," and your grandfather's laughter hints of the acceptance of her sexuality, and she goes on, "Quit laughing, I can barely control this fire hose as it is!" and you all laugh and are graced by the bonds flowing between you.

The day eventually passes and fades into the uncertainty of the night. You must go and let your grandfather get some sleep. In the excitement of today's togetherness, it was easy to forget that he was ill, but your anxiety creeps back in with the encroaching darkness. He appears uncomfortable again, but insists there's nothing anyone can do. He looks aged and unkempt. You must leave him alone until morning. This is not a usual parting; you are sorrowful because you are unsure, worried because you may never see him alive again. You are aware of the inadequacy of a simple *"good night."* You deliberately let everyone else exchange embraces until you and he are the only ones left in the room. You wonder what words could possibly summarize your feelings, how you could articulate an ocean of sentiment. He is returning your poignant stare and you note that through a lifetime the eyes go unchanged, that skin will wrinkle and sag, hair will thin and gray, but that eyes in old age are the same as they are in youth. You see yourself in him as he lies there, separated only by a greater wear of years.

He breaks the silence and says, "I'm so glad to see you looking as good as you do. It's an absolute hell to be this sick and I know that you went through a lot worse than I am now, and for a lot longer. I didn't even come to visit you in the hospital, I was so busy running around."

"It's okay, Gramp. I know exactly how you feel," you say, speaking both of illness and regret, hearing his apology. You hold his hand. You have never felt closer to him. Through the misery that binds you, you feel one of life's greatest joys. Your empathy is a conduit that takes you toward his soul, and he can feel the warmth of yours. You tell him that you love him and that he has brought a wealth of goodness into his tiny portion of the world. He then tells you that he loves you, but you hear the awkward unfamiliarity in his tremulous voice, the difficulty that proud men have in articulating a feeling for the first time.

The next morning you walk nervously down the hospital hallway with your father and sister, not knowing if you'll find your grandfather in bed or if you'll be weeping in an empty room. You see his nurse outside his door and she says that he has entered a very deep sleep during the night, not unlike a coma. Hannah and Suki are already beside him, you can see that they've been crying. Your appearance is a catalyst for even more tears. Your grandfather is catatonic. His mouth is hanging open and his every breath is frightfully prolonged and labored. It is very difficult to see him like this. He is unresponsive to touch and sound. He has fallen over that dark edge. You are haunted, terrified. You are looking at it. This could have been your death too. You remember the gurgled breathing. In looking at his blanched body you see your own immobility, the motionlessness of a corpse. You are looking at the nearly indistinguishable division that separates decrepitude from death. He is fading like an ember. He is slipping into the blackness. Now he has gone further than you had to go.

The day is spent in waiting. With little motion and little noise your family sits and watches the flesh of his chest slowly rise, as if climbing, and then fall like an autumn leaf in the calm. You wonder where he is. Whispers of love are told to his ear in hopes that he can still be reached. And the cruel afternoon gives way to the peace of the night when it finally comes. There is a pause in his breathing and then an extremely deep breath as though he is preparing to speak. This is death, where life's remaining seconds can be counted by a child. Then, in the thickness of the silence, as he harnesses every last bit of strength, one final unsteady intake of air that he holds until gravity causes it to seep from his body.

* * *

As the poet is forgiving of the sunset on clouded and rainy

days, so too do you forgive in eulogy. You share the vast scope of color that his aura created, grand remembrances to offset the weighted pain of loss. All that adored him, all that called him friend are sitting before you in congregation, those for whom he cared, those with whom he laughed, those that he had silently loved. You paint the portrait that allows release, and, in that deluge of joy and sorrow, a community is bound together. You touch the sentiments that surround life's journey, of the misery and of the bliss, and as you speak a crowd of people cries because a young man is still alive and because an old man has passed away.

∞

3   A Mother's Perspective

I am blessed with two wonderful children—polar opposites. Josh, my first born, is a private person, a solitary man. Comfortable with himself and unconcerned with what others think, he remains a nonconformist, secure in his own identity. He loves the outdoors, whether cross-country skiing, canoeing, camping or traveling. His wanderlust for new places and new people feeds his soul. He has a brilliant mind, sharp as a razor, a quick wit and a poet's way with words.

Julie, three years younger than her brother is a blond-haired, brown-eyed imp—headstrong since birth. Never one to be left behind, she constantly tagged after her big brother. She shunned dolls and refused to don frilly dresses—a tomboy with an athlete's grace. With her outgoing, bubbly personality she has a multitude of friends. Creative, intuitive and talented, she loves sports and excells in volleyball. She idolizes her big brother.

I never knew that their lives were about to become even more intricately entwined.

Life came to a standstill one fateful day in February, shattering my world and altering my life forever. On Valentine's Day, 1994 I received a devastating phone call from my twenty-five year old son. I was stunned! The doctor must have made a mistake in his diagnosis; my son couldn't possibly have leukemia. He'd never been sick a day in his life. I had just spent Christmas with him and his sister and he was quite healthy—tall and lean with a ravenous appetite and sporting a shaggy head of dark brown hair and full beard. *My son can't possibly have AML!* The words acute myelogenous leukemia altered my world forever.

Flying to his bedside in a daze, I remember little of the journey. My focus was to reach my son. Illness of this magnitude had never struck my family, and I soon realized I was not exempt from this deadly game of Russian roulette. Comprehension dawned as I stepped off the fourth floor elevator at the medical center and saw the sign "Cancer Disorders." Reality hit with stunning force. The big "C"! A death sentence. My tears fell once again.

I don't remember my first words to him, but as we hugged tightly, I remember thinking, *just give him what he needs to get well and get us out of here.* This attitude remained steadfast throughout each treatment, wavering only slightly each time the doctors re-assessed the situation and repeated their grim prognosis. No one expected him to survive.

Only once did he ask, "Why me, Mom?" Of course, there is no answer. All I could do was push forward with optimism and encouragement. Medical breakthroughs and cures are discovered every day. There are always alternatives and choices.

I don't believe I ever fully understood the meaning of parenthood until I became a parent myself. While growing up, did I really understand my parents—their feelings and struggles? Did I look at them as individuals? Or were they simply "Mom and Dad"—my safety net, my source of unconditional love. Their loving arms were always there to catch me when I fell. And nothing is more reassuring than a mother's embrace—a remedy as reliable as chicken soup.

Parental worry is seeded at birth and lasts a lifetime. From kindergarten through college, each challenge is met. After graduation, job selection and marriage, you begin to think you can finally breathe a little easier and enjoy the fruits of your labor before grandchildren arrive.

But here I am, facing the greatest challenge of my life. I am unprepared. With no nursing skills or medical training, I am about to get a crash course in *Nursing 101*—a course I do not want and cannot fail. Unfamiliar terms—*CBC, Aracee, Zofran, Ativan, Neupogen, Vancomycin, Allopurinol, Coreg, Digoxin, Tegaderm, saline, Heparin, Ampho-B, Hickman*—become part of my everyday vocabulary and the hospital protocol and procedures all too familiar. My son's every bodily function is strictly monitored. Forever lost are modesty and privacy.

I must be strong. I cannot crumble for I have a new job. I am *Nurse*. I can endure anything because nothing is more important than my son's well being. I can cope with any extraneous force—an ex-husband; his new wife and stepchildren; unfamiliar surroundings; leaving my job and new-found friends; uprooting myself and my daughter yet again—to ensure that my son's delicate frame of mind is kept on an even keel and his energy focused on getting well. With his innate intuitiveness he will detect negative vibes or familial discord. I am relentless, but I have no control. I have taken care of him for most of his life, and now his care is in the hands of strangers. It is, without a doubt, the most stressful time of my life.

As I sit beside his hospital bed, a maelstrom of emotions assail me. I am helpless. There is nothing I can do. I must rely totally on the expertise of the medical personnel to save his life while poisoning his system with the chemicals running through the tubes attached to his body.

I have no knowledge of the disease that attacks him. I have no magic wand to wave, nor do I have control over the critical decisions essential to his care. I am a sounding board. He is an adult, capable of making solid, sensible decisions as has been his custom long before his departure for college. Josh quizzes and questions the doctors, weighing all recommendations and alternatives. Then he decides. It is his body, his life. He knows what's best. I trust him to make the right decision.

Yet I am paralyzed with fear he won't survive. I am floating, suspended in time as the days slowly drift by.

As I live through each traumatic event and watch the scene unfold, I realize each of us has a defined role in this unscripted drama—family, friends, girlfriend, doctors, nurses and fraternity brothers. Each suffers and grieves privately. Each has strength to impart and we are all paramount to his recovery.

My role is simple yet complex. I am where I want to be. I am where I need to be—by his side. For purely selfish reasons, I feel better and more calm when I am near, where I can touch; where I can see and watch with an eagle's eye for any sign of change.

Though I feel totally useless, I offer my strength with a gentle touch, a kiss to the brow, a smile—always supporting him through my daily bedside vigil, chasing away his fears and nursing him back to health. I don't like leaving, however briefly, as I am afraid something will happen while I'm gone—a medication might be forgotten or he'll be given the wrong one. Or he might need immediate help with the vomit pan, the urinal, or want a tasty snack or a cool drink. The nursing staff is often overloaded with patients, and pressing the call button doesn't always bring a quick response. I don't want him to wait a second longer than necessary. Fully gowned, masked and wearing rubber gloves, I am there.

I watch as he fights the oxygen mask covering his nose and mouth as he struggles to breathe; I watch as he vomits uncontrollably from the chemicals that poison his system; I watch as he tosses and turns, delirious with fever and packed in ice; and I watch his hair fall out by the handful and the weight melt off his once-strong, six feet five inch frame. He changes daily before my eyes. He is skeletal—so fragile, lying curled in a fetal position. He never utters a complaint. He is my strength. If he can endure these atrocities, so can I. He is so frightened. So am I. But his fears are held within. We do not discuss the possibility of death. But I am there.

My daughter Julie offers her unwavering belief that recovery is imminent. I remember my elation when I learned she was a bone marrow match—many patients often die before finding a donor. She screamed with delight and ran through the hospital corridors shouting with glee, literally jumping for joy. As her body was tested, poked and prodded, she maintained her wit and sense of humor, and readily welcomed the opportunity to offer her bone marrow to save her brother's life. Her refreshing, upbeat attitude was a welcome reprieve from the sombre tone permeating our lives. Her belief in her brother's survival was absolute; her fears were silent.

To have both my children endure the bone marrow harvest and transplant while lying in separate hospitals is doubly difficult. I am torn. Where should my vigil be? I know the risks of anesthesia and am concerned for my daughter's welfare. What if something goes wrong? I could lose both of my children! With herculeon effort, I ignore my panic, knowing her gift far outweighs any risk. But I am so afraid.

I wish they could have been in beds next to each other so I could watch over them both; so Julie could watch her marrow slowly drip into her brother's body and witness his smile of admiration, gratitude and love. But the reality is harsh—Josh is alone in a sterile environment, his immune system destroyed by preparations for the transplant. Julie, equally prepped and medicated, lies in a hospital across the street, dozing intermittently as the nausea and severe headaches in reaction to the anesthesia begin to ease. She has seventeen harvest sites and over two hundred puncture wounds in her lower back. Only telephone access is permitted.

His father, Jim, is tenacious in his endless search for alternatives—new treatments, new doctors, nutrition supplements and homeopathic options. He is perpetual motion and out of his element sitting in a hospital room. His strength lies elsewhere—he is a doer, a solver of problems who is unable to help his own son. Devastated, he battles his own private demons. For him, facing the possibility of his son's death is unthinkable. He is in denial.

With her youthful exuberance, Josh's girlfriend Jody brightens the endless hours. She is friend, lover and confidante packaged in five feet seven inches of boundless energy. Her bond is special—she is in love. It warms my heart to witness the joy they bring to each other, for she makes him feel like a man despite an emasculating disease.

Mail delivery has become a daily delight. It is always a wonderful surprise to receive a box of goodies or a handful of cards. I am overwhelmed by the generosity of family, friends and the community at large—by the multitude of cards, phone calls, visits and packages of good cheer. Their expressions of support are truly appreciated and their love comforts me throughout the endless days of confinement. There isn't much to say, but then, no words are necessary.

Due to rotating schedules, the doctors and nurses constantly change. Dedicated professionals, each differs in their bedside manner, their opinion and their attitude. Some are gentle, some are not. Some are patient, some are not. Some are sympathetic, some are not. I expect their honesty but desperately need their encouragement. How can they deliver such grim prognoses, see the heartbreaking waste, feel the desolation and not be affected? How can they touch my son, see the daily changes and not weep? It must ravage their souls. It devastates mine.

Countless fraternity brothers are in daily contact, lending moral support and wishes for a speedy recovery—Johnny, Eric, Mark, Glen, Jim, Will, Pete, Rob, Don, Dave, Mike ... there are so many I forget all their names. I am amazed, but not surprised, by the staunch support, loyalty and strength of this group of young men who epitomize the meaning of brotherhood. Who knows the youthful "hell" they endured, what death defying feats

Sigma Pi Brothers (Josh in foreground)

they shared to form this unbreakable bond, but a finer group of young men I will never know. Not unlike the domino effect, when one knows, they all know what is happening to their "brother." From across the country, they call and reminisce about their college antics, or come to visit and, on occasion, spring him from his hospital cell for a few hours to enjoy a picnic in the park. While envious, Josh is content to watch his buddies toss the frisbee or guzzle a few beers. Although he lacks the physical strength to join in the fun, he is extremely grateful to be outside under the sunny, blue sky enjoying the camaraderie of his friends. What better medicine than laughter and friends!

Myriad thoughts flit through my mind during the long, lonely hours. It's a time of solitude, a quiet moment to reflect on the carefree days of their childhood. I vividly recall every athletic triumph on the basketball or volleyball court, the baseball or hockey field. I wonder how many hours I logged sitting on hard bleachers on cold and blustery days, or cheering their efforts while crammed inside a sweaty gym. How many hours did I spend driving or car pooling to and from swimming lessons, after school activities or sleepovers with friends? I also recall the plays and the proms, the battle to get them to take dancing lessons. I remember how I swelled with pride watching them grow from gangly, awkward children into graceful athletes and beautiful young adults. With a loving hand, I tried to impart life's important lessons.

Junior Prom, 1985

I cherish those carefree days of their childhood. How precious the moments of each first word, first step, first tooth! I fondly remember being awakened in the pre-dawn hours of Christmas morn to watch their delight in unwrapping the goodies Santa had brought. It was such a glorious time, but where did it go? Through tears of joy I remember it all and cherish every minute, every tear, as I await his recovery.

* * *

No matter where I am or where I go, Josh is never far from my thoughts. And, yes, I have mentally planned his funeral on more than one occasion. These unwanted thoughts creep into my mind when I least expect it and, enraged, I quickly shove them aside. I have worked too hard ensuring the quality of his care to give up. I know he has a potentially fatal disease, but I remain optimistic.

Josh, Julie and Santa, 1974

It's been two years since the initial diagnosis. Josh has endured three relapses, countless rounds of chemotherapy, a bone marrow transplant and two T-cell infusions.

With each relapse, I find coping more difficult ... coping on good days is tolerable, on bad days unbearable. My fears deepen and nothing can alleviate them. I feel I am sitting on a keg of dynamite. I momentarily falter, allowing the anxiety to surface, bringing with it depression and despair. I survived on adrenaline for so many months but crash emotionally when I am alone. I want so desperately to return to the mundane chores of everyday life, but cannot. I know nothing will ever be the same again. My days are random. Some days I have no energy; some days I seek the familiarity of a tennis game with friends; and some days I need solitude. My life is irrevocably altered.

Whenever Josh calls I initially panic, for it's not his habit to call. It always takes a few heart-stopping seconds before my heart resumes its normal rhythm. I am hovering, smothering and suffocating him with my endless queries regarding his health. There's not an hour in the day that I don't think about him. I am frightened. I watch him struggle, trying to come to grips with his own mortality. It is heartbreaking. He pushes forward relentlessly, doing the things he loves and making plans for the future. He has a life to live! I can only wait and pray, anxiously awaiting the results of each CBC, holding my breath in fear of bad news, and only breathing a sigh of relief when the counts are normal. I watch as he continually searches for the healing benefits of good nutrition, special vitamin supplements and macrobiotic alternatives. I watch him cherish each day. I watch. That is all I can do. He is scared. He is weary of treatments and wants his life back.

To reassure myself, I continue the weekly calls to my children, just hearing their voices boosts my spirits. I find, too, that I need to see them more often, once or twice a year is simply not enough. I need their touch, their hugs and kisses to maintain my sanity. The moments of laughter and tears bind us closer, giving us a new outlook on life and, most importantly, a deeper appreciation of one other.

Life is very precious—a fact I never truly realized until this tragedy befell. Today I savor every moment. Each day is different. Each day is unique. I inhale the beauty and tranquility of nature. I wrap myself in comforting sights and serene sounds ... flickering candlelight, soft music, gentle waves rushing to the shore, brilliant sunsets and twinkling stars on a moonlit night. I simply take one day at a time.

And if this disease rears its ugly head again, all of us will do what we have done before—extend all our love and support, hoping for another reprieve and always smiling through our fears. The strength to conquer this disease lies in our unity. He is not alone, the disease attacks us all.

With the strength of prayer, the potency of a positive mental attitude and the salvation of a sense of humor, he will survive.

∞

4 Donor Experience

Being the bone marrow donor for my brother, my only sibling, was the most emotionally draining, physically painful and exhausting thing I have ever done in my life. From the moment Josh was diagnosed with leukemia I knew we would match and he would be fine. The idea of his death never entered my mind. It would be my crowning achievement. I would be his savior. The hospital stays, radiation and chemotherapy were all steps along the way, things we had to do to survive. Things certainly were not what I thought and did not turn out the way I had hoped or expected.

From day one, Josh was always my hero and totally invulnerable. He was the oldest and was not interested in his pesky little sister. He resented my forced presence. Being isolated on the farm, all we had was each other. We played together in the barn, on the pond, in the creek and in the apple orchard. Countless bruises and scratches left their mark.

Regardless of his hatred for me, I tagged along and did all the "boy" things he wanted to do. Sledding, skiing, building hay forts in the barn, strapping ourselves to the huge hay feeder and rolling each other down the corn fields, bike riding down Cush Hill, catching salamanders and frogs and apple throwing wars in the orchard were among our favorite pastimes. He loved to pelt me with apples from the treetops or from the ground. Boy how they stung! But I would endure, as I would do anything to be with my big brother.

As with any sibling rivalry, Josh and I never really got along until he went away to college. I visited him a couple of times at St. Lawrence University. We had a blast! He tucked me under his wing, introduced me to all his fraternity brothers and took me to parties. We went a little crazy and had so much fun. On his trips home I still followed him around because I wanted to be with him all the time.

We grew even closer as I, too, headed off to college. He visited me at the University of Vermont, helped me move into my dorm and, after graduation, moved me home again in August 1993 where we shared a duplex house. We saw each other all the time. Our relationship continued to grow and we became friends. We played cards, went to parties and just simply enjoyed each other's company. We had a great time until he became sick less than a year later on February 14, 1994.

From that fateful day on and for the next four years, all of our lives were put on hold. A friend of mine was living out in California and I was heading out there to live. Three weeks before the flight Josh was diagnosed with leukemia. My move was cancelled.

The first day in the hospital we met all of Josh's doctors and they said to me, "We are going to come looking for you," which terrified me. The doctors explained that siblings have the best chance of being a match for a bone marrow transplant. The day we found out I was a match, I screamed with joy and could have been heard all the way back in Sherburne, two hours away. My role was set. I would donate my marrow. I would be the hero. I would save his life. Everyone was so happy and proud of me. It was a cause for celebration and filled me with joy and optimism.

The Webb entourage practically lived at the hospital everyday from nine in the morning until nine at night. The words "visiting hours" did not apply to us. We came and went as we pleased. It became a new way of life. We knew everything ... where to get the ice, drinks and clean sheets, where the cleanest restrooms were, which nurses we liked, who we wanted to take care of Josh and what time the doctors made their rounds. We monitored all his meds, knew their purpose and when he needed them. We held his urinals, wiped his butt and fed him his meals.

We played thousands of games including twelve-point pitch, hearts, dominoes, *Scattergories* and, my favorite, *Scrabble*™, which I played with either Mom or Dad because Josh hated it. We played with Josh when he was awake and played with each other while he slept. Mom read hundreds of books, Dad continued to work and I stitched or crocheted numerous projects. We watched countless episodes of the Simpsons, Wheel of Fortune and Jeopardy. But our favorite activity was EATING! Going to lunch or dinner was a tiny, daily escape. We also had to get Josh some edible food as the hospital food was simply gross. In Syracuse our favorite hangout was the *Bagel Diner*. We spent so much time with the owners and got to know them so well that they came to Josh's funeral.

Our hospital stays were long and frustrating, but oddly enough filled with laughter. We were on an emotional roller coaster and trapped in our room, a tiny cramped cell.

My positive attitude was unshakable as I firmly believed he would recover. Perhaps it was my innocence, my naiveté or just my strong belief that he would live. My brother was just too strong to be taken from us. His physical strength, great attitude and youth were all on his side. Nothing would stop him! The bone marrow transplant would work! I was never afraid of losing him because I knew my marrow would save his life.

The process of the transplant began and I voiced plenty of complaints about it. With my fear of needles, becoming a human pincushion was certainly not appealing. It was my job to complain and constantly remind him of my sacrifices. After all, I was his chance for becoming healthy again.

The entire process of the bone marrow transplant was hard on everyone involved. Josh had to undergo extensive chemo and radiation treatments and was literally locked in his room for a month, leaving only for his radiation treatments. My part was easy compared to what Josh had to do.

The doctors explained that the bone marrow extraction was a relatively simple procedure and that my body would replenish its own marrow. I would have no ill effects. So waking up in the recovery room in intense pain was not something I had anticipated. The surgery left seventeen harvest sites in my lower back about the size of a pea and over two hundred holes in my hip bone where they removed over one liter of fluid. Sitting up in bed was difficult. Walking to the bathroom was impossible. The anesthesia made me sick. I vomited three times, aggravating the pain in my back. Food was totally unappealing and sleep was my number one priority. Mom, Dad, and my friend, Lisa, came to see me in my hospital room where I remained overnight.

Within an hour after the marrow was aspirated, it was given to Josh while I still lay in a numbed, drugged state. He called me on the phone from his room when he was receiving the marrow through his IV and said, "They're yummy!"—something we always said when he received any kind of blood products. It took him about five minutes to receive over one billion of my cells. I still have the little plastic bag they came in as a memento.

After the doctors released me from the hospital and with my back covered in bandages, I made a quick visit to see Josh before heading back to the apartment where we were staying. Josh laughed at me as I stumbled into his room. I looked horrible! As the harvest totally wiped me out, it took two days of sleep before I felt like myself again, but even then I was not fully recovered. The harvest was a very unpleasant experience, but one I would have endured again.

Watching Josh live his life over the next few months was inspiring. Seeing him everyday made my experience so much more satisfying ... just seeing him healthy and enjoying life again. Josh embraced life. He was so courageous, so adventurous.

He did everything humanly possible to improve the quality of his life. He searched for new ways to help his own immune system fight the blast cells, consulted non-traditional doctors and investigated various types of holistic treatments, including coffee enemas, carrot juice, shark cartilage injections, detoxification and green tea. Every new treatment he discovered, he tried.

One of my most treasured memories of that time was when Josh gave a most incredible speech at my grandfather Webb's funeral. (Gramp died two weeks after Josh was released from the hospital following his transplant.) Completely bald and wearing his protective mask, the sight of his six feet five inch skin-and-bones frame walking to the pulpit was enough to make everyone in the church weep. While at the podium, he took off his mask and spoke eloquently of his love and admiration for our grandfather. His eulogy touched everyone's heart. There was not a dry eye in the church.

My time as his savior was short-lived, as Josh relapsed after fourteen healthy months. I was devastated that he did not want to try a second bone marrow transplant. I wanted to help him again. Being his donor made me feel special, but it was his decision.

Supporting Josh was our goal. I realized that being on the entertainment squad and being there for my mother as well as my brother was just as important as being the donor. It was paramount that we—Mom, Jody, and I—be there for each other. We all contributed our strengths and helped each other get through each day and remain sane.

Josh, Grandma Webb and Julie after Grandpa Webb's funeral.

The doctor told him, "Pack up your tent and maybe have a nice summer," but he was not going to give up that easily. Other doctors wanted to do another bone marrow transplant but it was all Josh could do to endure the first one, let alone a second. Once was enough! Instead of a second transplant, he chose to receive my T-cells, attempted on two separate occasions. Neither of these infusions worked.

Instead, Josh elected to try a new and unproven chemo regimen that damaged his body so badly he could not recover. His heart and lungs became infected and, for a long time, he was so weak he could not walk and was confined to a wheelchair. During this time, Josh took a trip that I will never forget.

The volleyball team I coached was playing in Rochester in September of 1997. Josh rarely came to see me play, let alone any

Always the Big Brother

of the teams that I coached, so when he decided to come and watch the team I was elated.

Josh had just gotten out of the hospital again and was still in recovery mode. My parents packed his wheelchair, oxygen tanks and medications, loaded him into the car and drove to the university tournament site. It was a momentous occasion when he was wheeled into the gym. It was the highlight of my year as he made his entrance and sat in his wheelchair across the court from us. Our team lost the match in a very close 13-15 deciding fifth game, and afterwards he said that if we had won he was going to walk across the gym and give me a hug, which would have reduced me to a bout of fresh tears. Josh and my parents stayed for only one match for Josh was tiring and they had a two-hour trip home. As I watched them leave, the tears rolled down my cheeks. Josh went above and beyond expectations to support me. I will never forget the way he looked as he sat in his wheelchair across the gym from me.

Getting ready for Christmas was very difficult. We all went overboard on our gift selections. It was very lavish and we had a blast! It took us hours to individually open all our gifts. Josh's arms were so swollen that he could barely manage the task. He never got off the couch. Watching him open his gifts with his comical facial expressions was as important as the gift. At the end of the day we all stood together for our last portrait in front of the Christmas tree.

New Year's Eve was also traumatic when we rushed Josh to the emergency room for an IV Demerol. In that little emergency room, we all cried as the doctors told us the blast cells had returned. I remember Josh saying to Jody, "I'm going to make you a widow before we even get married." Thank God we had each other.

My holiday break from work was soon over and the time to say good-bye had come. That night, the tears came again and facing Josh was unbearable. In the morning, as soon as Mom walked into the kitchen, I burst into tears and said, "I don't want to go." I was crying hysterically, but Josh was waiting for his hug good-bye. Mom made Jody and me pose for a picture with him, all three of us lying on his bed. My eyes were closed and my face was red and tear-stained. We hugged and I told him I would see him next weekend. Leaving was unbearable.

I made a quick trip home to Pittsburgh to take care of things and then returned to New York with funeral attire in hand. I arrived on Friday night, January 30. When I got home, Josh was in his usual position lying on the couch with his arms folded on his chest. Reverend Steve was there and Dad was sitting on the end of the couch rubbing Josh's red-speckled, swollen feet. The fire was blazing while we reminisced and, of course, laughed and laughed. After everyone left and Josh went to bed, I went out for a little while to meet some friends and when I returned Josh was screaming in agony. Mom tried to give him some Demerol but it would not stay down. His screams were hard to bear as they echoed inside of my head. We were sitting on his bed when he put his hand on top of mine and looked at me with such a feeling of love, pain and exhaustion on his face that words were not needed. There was nothing to say. I couldn't bear watching him twist in agony or listen to his cries of pain so I went to bed and put a pillow over my head. I barely slept that night. The next morning, Mom came into my bedroom in tears to say we were going to the hospital.

That day, January 31, 1998, will forever be embedded in my memory. When we arrived at the hospital, I told Mom that it was not "the day," but I was wrong. There was nothing the medical staff could do for him except to make him comfortable. Josh made jokes and was himself to the end, saying to the doctor, "They're just waiting for me to kick the bucket." As we all held hands around his bed, watching his heart rate slow, Reverend Steve prayed aloud and it was then I realized Josh was going to die. I panicked! I was not ready! I had not come to grips with this at all. How could this happen? My big brother was invincible!

The Demerol eased his pain, while his breathing grew slower and his breaths further apart. There was little we could do for him now except soothe him by holding his hand, putting a cool towel on his head and rubbing his red, swollen arms. I sat on the side of the bed with Mom hugging me tight as we waited.

"Hey, it's me—your sister," I said between sobs. After that, my exact words were unclear, but I tried to tell him that as much as I complained about the bone marrow transplant, I wished I could have done it again. I told him that I loved him very much. I hope he heard me—it was one of the few times the words *I love you* ever came out of my mouth.

His breathing slowed, each breath further and further apart until they finally stopped. It seemed like forever. Then he was gone. He was now free from the leukemia—free from the pain. Reverend Steve said, "Josh will always have a part of you with him in the bone marrow," a thought still brings me comfort. But the image of him lying lifeless in his hospital bed will never leave my mind. It is as clear to me today as it was then—and as it will be for the rest of my life.

Josh had so much courage and lived without fear, which serves as a huge inspiration for me. Everyone loved and admired him for being such a wonderful person. Josh always treated people with respect and was genuinely interested in them and what they had to say. He paid attention to you and made you feel special. He taught me so much, especially, that we must cherish every day.

There is no more tragic way to learn this lesson. I lost my brother when he was not yet years thirty years old. Time goes by quickly, and if we don't stop to enjoy life and do the things we want to do, time will run out. It scared me. I needed to do something about my stagnant life or I was certainly going to disappoint him. Josh's life and death inspires me to become the best person I can possibly be and to live life to its fullest.

He touched so many people in his unforgettable way—what more tangible proof than all those who attended his funeral, the countless number who called, the hundreds who sent cards and the many who sent the most beautiful plants and flowers. All the kind words and memorable stories related at his funeral amazed me. His two-hour funeral service was a beautiful celebration of his life and a true testimony to his greatness.

What saddens me the most is that the one person who really knew me, witnessed every aspect of my life, was gone. My future husband and my unborn children will not be able to know this person who was such an unforgettable force in my life. It is a tragedy and yet a challenge for the rest of us to keep his legacy alive through his stories and our memories—he was too special to simply fade away.

∞

5 Relapse

In the voice of one fraternity brother, Josh writes of the fear this brother faces as he watches his vital young friend's life fade, and of the guilt impossible to keep at bay.

I became a geologist because I am fascinated by rocks, not because I want to stand next to a cacophonous drilling rig in order to verify that blue-collar rummies are doing their work. When I landed this job, I thought I had hit the big time. I am a Geodynamic and Hydrostatic Engineer. I fill out paperwork. I am a non-participant, a drone. My job is little more than a safeguard against liability suits. It's a big company. When it rains, I watch from the cab of the truck while men perform their duties, and I kill time by making intermittent scratches in my notebook. Nine, ten hours a day, often until dark. Sometimes I supervise the sewage jobs ... leech fields, drainage. Our clients are industrial-scale: shopping malls, power plants. I am the only "college boy" in the field. The hardened, middle-aged laborers are decent people, we have lunch together, but there is a chasm between us. They have different amusements. I cannot converse convincingly about an approaching sport season. I occasionally wonder if they're poking fun at me. They know that I don't get dirty, that I make more money than I deserve. I confirm that the back hoe operator has dug deep enough. Two college degrees and I make pencil X's in boxes. My checklists go straight into file, I could cover them with nursery rhymes. I feel as useful as an appendix. Ten months of this and I am already numb.

I don't know if a slow death is better than a fast one. All this digging in the earth and I see graves.

Like any education, I merely had textbook conceptions of disease until I had the misfortune of firsthand experience. I was two thousand miles away when he was originally diagnosed and, though the news was shocking, the disagreeable emotions resting beside a vivid prospect of death were never stirred. I was callously nonchalant. I knew that he would recover. He was the kind of person that always won. He was athletic and intelligent. He was enviably spirited. Beating leukemia would be something else that he was good at. My powers of imagination were sadly inadequate in comprehending his turmoil. The extent of my empathy consisted of the realization that daily vomiting must have been unpleasant. I didn't have time for idle reflections or sentimental get-well cards. I was chasing the tail of routine, occupied with my studies, and to know him was to be unalarmed. Mutual friends reported that he was handling the treatment well. His disease was only a minor aberration in an order soon to be restored. My certainty in his recovery clipped any tendril of sorrow before it could creep in. I thought of his illness as an inconvenience for him. It was only troubling because if it could happen to him it could happen to anyone.

After I received my master's degree, I accepted my job in the Northeast and was able to see him again. By then he was back to normal. He looked like he had never had anything wrong with him. He was lively and robust. He recollected his disease with a tone of shell shock, but it was in the past, it was over. Life went on as usual. We saw each other about once a month, we would go mountain biking or drink a few beers. It was great to be in his company again, I devoted more thanks to my relocation than to his recovery. I was thankful to be near my friend, he was fun, he was kind, he helped lift me out my occupational doldrums. I took his health for granted. I thought a bone marrow transplant was a cure. I didn't know that he could have a relapse.

I had taken Friday off from work so that the two of us could go canoeing for the weekend. I had a four hour drive to his place that morning. He had mentioned something about a one-year check-up. He said later that he had tried to call me to stop me from coming, but I had already been on my way. When I arrived I noticed that the canoe was not loaded on his truck. His girlfriend Jody's car was in the driveway and she was supposed to be at work. The scene was not as it should have been. I gave a quick knock on the door and let myself in. He was lying on the couch with his head in Jody's lap. Her face was streaked with tears and she was stroking his hair, each caress assuring him of her love, confirming for her that he was still there. His eyes were swollen with crying. There was no customary greeting. His dog Siska even looked depressed. My inertia dropped to the floor as I began to piece together what was happening. He stood up and choked out, "Leukemia's got me again," as he wrapped his arms around me. I felt the weight of his body upon me. He wet my shoulder with his tears. He convulsed with sorrow. I had no preparation for this. Coldness came like a change of seasons. The extremity of his pain was foreign to me. I was no longer 2000 miles away, I felt the frantic pounding of his heart against my chest, cast immediately beside the rawness of his fear of dying.

This wreckage was savage and rank, completely contrary to my gleeful expectations. Standing in his arms his pain was a contagion.

I felt the violation accompanying the force of such cruelty, the wrongness, the indignation for the threatened thievery of his life. In that torrent of agony, I was silenced by the shock. My sense of decency commanded a response yet words escaped me. I had no bearings in this downpour of despair. I was face down in the mud, grasping in gloomy, tractionless bewilderment. I didn't know how to reach him. I felt the voiceless impotence of nightmares. I experienced pinpricking and sensations of nausea. I had brief and fanciful denials of this new reality. His devastation radiated outwardly, he was the epicenter of a human calamity, falling to pieces, filled with disease. His structure toppled. He sat down and cried with mayhem and hysteria. His soul ached and moaned. I thanked God that I was not him. I had never seen him shed tears before. It was like experiencing a hurricane without ever knowing rain. I stared at him like a monstrosity. I felt terrible for him. I fumbled through trite sympathies and consolations, unversed in the language of commiseration. I felt uncomfortable and out of place. Conversation was impossible. The normal cues of interaction had disappeared in the wash of catastrophe. I was dumbfounded. I wanted to be supportive but I was running into a barrier. He was trapped alone inside a bubble. As he wilted with sobbing, Jody sadly whispered that the doctors wanted him to start chemo on Monday. They had the audacity to tell him that his odds were only twenty percent. Until that point in our lives our relationship had been that of children, we had been playmates, we had laughed together, we had experienced initiations, we had been drunken bugs giggling under the moon and stars. Life finally reared its ugly head. The bottom fell out of our former denominators. I barely recognized the person in ruins before me. The thickness of his agony was suffocating. I was cornered by a terror that I couldn't fight, which kindness wouldn't allow me to flee. Never had the duties implicit in true friendship been placed so vividly before me. I sought security in, "Is there anything that I can do?" It was something that I knew friends said. He asked me to stay with him for the weekend and, with weighted resignation, I solemnly conceded.

I have always lived a sheltered life. There is no classroom for an education in fear and dying. The everyday reminders of mortality are few and abrupt. Once I killed a dog that ran in front of my car, another time I stumbled upon a stinking deer carcass in the forest. Human death is masked, hidden in euphemisms and make-up. Interminable separation is cloaked with otherworldly reunion. We only learn the pain when we have to face it. Only one of my grandparents is dead and when that happened my parents kept it from me, I was just a child. Grandpa was probably ready to die anyway. Age acquiesces. Youth is different. Youth will rage and kick and claw. My friend's world of possibilities dimmed and narrowed until it looked like the inside of a small wooden box. He was squeezed on one side by a body riddled with disease and on the other side by toxic therapy and incarceration. The first time he was blissfully ignorant of what he had to face, this time he knew it all too well.

He agonized over informing his parents. He knew, of course, that he had to do it, but it tore him apart like the cancer within him. He hated putting them through the trauma, he saw how it crushed them the last time, watching helplessly while their child contorted with nausea and fever. I sat with him in the living room as he made the phone calls. His father cried so loudly that my friend had to hold the receiver away from his ear. He winced in sadness and he shook his head as if he just wanted it all to stop. He couldn't believe it was happening again. Jody was sitting next to me and she began crying when she saw his tears and she grabbed my hand and I tried to convey empathy in the tightening of my grip. I was immersed in their tragedy. I was flooded in their otherwise private woe. My friend eventually calmed down enough to inform his father of the medical agenda. He was going to have a Hickman catheter implanted in his chest at eight o'clock on Monday. A CAT scan was to follow later in the morning and then he was to begin his chemotherapy protocol sometime in the afternoon, dripped into his veins over a one week period, then the following week his immune system would crash and he would enter the period of vulnerability. In another couple of weeks he would recover enough to be released. That was the best-case scenario. If everything went well, he'd be out of the hospital in a month. That's what they told him last time and it took nine weeks. Depending on how he handled the treatment, he might have more chemo and then a second transplant in three or four months, which would be another ordeal. He called his mother and broke the news; he waited weeping while she went to throw up. He told her the dreaded schedule of events through the same strangulation of tears. She would try to fly in on Sunday evening. He said that would be soon enough. He called his sister wondering if he could have more marrow if needed, saying that he was sorry and that he didn't know what he would do without her. He told her the details and they wept, then he hung up the phone. His family had been walking without worry when the shock waves collapsed their whole world on a Friday afternoon.

He fell into a cushioned chair like he had just completed a marathon. He was emotionally exhausted. He rested his head on the upholstery. He had been crying for three or four hours and his trial had really just begun. He gazed out the window. Every minute that passed brought him closer to losing his freedom and maybe his life. He couldn't get off the conveyor. He was the captive of a cruel fate. I could only begin to imagine his turmoil. He cried unabashedly. There was no false bravado. He was scared. His face grimaced as if he were being assailed, he wrapped his arms around his head in a strange configuration like slow moving snakes as if he was trying to keep his mind from bursting. He rocked back and forth, caught between boundaries with no options. He whined softly. He looked mentally ill, as if confined to a corner in a lonely asylum. His agony caused his behavior to warp beyond the rules of convention. This was a man who was normally very composed and jovial, who I often went to for advice. I was overwhelmed by a sense of the pressure that caused him to metamorphose. I was held in a ghastly trance, I was riveted, my heart ached for him, yet I could offer him no comfort, no embrace, no tear. His deviations arrested me. I was frozen. I stared at him like a beast in a cage with bars between us.

It is difficult to say exactly how we became friends. Proximity played a role, the necessary introduction of cramped freshman hall living, the random computer program that made the arrangements, predestining post-collegiate emotional lives. I remember the excited scramble for friends of college's first weekend, masking the underlying fear of solitude and being made an outcast. No one wanted to be alone, but the chemistry had to be right. There was a jumbled pool of vanities and jesters, styles, backgrounds, speech impediments, attitudes and varying degrees of likeability. The mechanisms of friendship are mysterious. Two minds, from vast possibilities, must make the same selection. My friend and I were somehow drawn to one another. We passed amiably through the customary hand shake and the myriad cues of the first impression. There were politely probing questions and exchanges of pre-tested humor. After this initial familiarization, a wonderful evolution occurred. As the days passed, bridges were formed between us. A multitude of diminutive events, from casual meals to doing laundry to playing baseball, all forged our relationship. This progression of bonds was unmappable, consisting of myriad reciprocations. Friendship is a kind of magic. It occurs at no definable moment. In the end there is security and acceptance. Friendship knows how vulnerable we are alone.

My friend and I complemented one another well. He was the dreamer and I was the realist, he was the romantic English major and I was the scientific geologist. Not that I was completely lacking in flights of passion or he in sensibility, but we balanced each other's deficiencies. He was more outgoing and this I admired, if there was one trait that I wanted to change in myself it was my reticence. He was articulate. He didn't have to nervously prepare for speeches and presentations. He could talk to women well. We both were attracted to the outdoors and we went camping frequently. We ventured in the wilderness because I loved studying rocky out croppings and he loved writing poetry about them. He would curiously watch me dislodging samples from some exposed cliff, chipping furiously with my rock hammer with dirt covering my face, interested in what made me tick, and I would catch glimpses of his extended silhouette reaching to the sky from some crag or hilltop, wondering the same of him. We had mutual respect, and this allowed us to joke about each other's distractions. We laughed about the differences in our modes of thinking, that I analyzed fragmented physical parts while he romanticized about the elusive whole. He kidded me about looking too closely, about falling in love with something as cold as granite. I kidded him about grandiose musings, about falling in love with intangibles. Yet he could appreciate my monologues on geological peculiarities, his questions indicated his interest and made me feel like an expert. I could appreciate his recitations of Coleridge and Blake, his aptitude causing me to ask for more.

He taught me that friendship is solidified when one feels the urge to defend. I remember distinctly the way I felt when I heard that he had defended me from the accusations of a belligerent football player who lived on our hall. Apparently the matter almost came to fists. I had a strong but vague awareness of our friendship until that point, but his defense of me crystallized my certainty, as if he had come out and said, "You are a dear friend, you mean a great deal to me, I will protect you." Not that we have ever talked about that event. Nor have we ever discussed our closeness. Our friendship is only tacitly understood, on visceral terms. Affection between men has never been a topic in vogue. Yet ours is a fallible system of understanding, open to confusions and self-doubt. My urge to defend my friend has manifested itself in silent ways. He has always preached seizing the day. This manifesto has brought him howling through the air as he jumped off cliffs and bridges into the water below. No platform was ever too high. Every time I watched I cringed, I wanted to protect him from his own foolish zeal. With a loud, *"Carpe Diem!"* he would hit the water and I would shake my head. After witnessing hundreds of these euphoric bursts of recklessness, whether plummeting into rivers or down ski slopes or on bicycles, I feared that the law of averages would catch up to him. It never did, and as he seemed immune to injury, I flirted with the idea of seizing some of that wild enthusiasm for myself. I wanted a taste of that energy. He had me talked into parachuting with him. He even got me to take the class, to put the chute on, and to go up in the plane with him. When I saw him let go of the strut of the wing and fall into the distance I thought, "no way." I couldn't jump into empty spaces. I realized then that he was just fundamentally more brave than I was. I saw his chute open. I was thankful that he wasn't killed. I rode the plane back to solid ground.

Ten minutes of silence passed, interrupted only by his groaning and gasps for air. I wanted to turn away, my insides churned as though I was being forced to view a film for which I had no disposition. The scene reeked with fear. It was polluted with horror. Only mildly calmed from his hysteria, he leveled me with the question, "Do you think I'm going to die?"

Immediately I was swept with nervousness, was thrown suddenly onto a foreign stage, unqualified, wanting to say the right words, fidgeting in the focus.

"You're not going to die!" cried Jody in reflexive rejection, as if his question was blasphemous, as if he was suggesting surrender.

"I might. I hate considering it, but I might. I might just die. Look at my reality ... a failed bone marrow transplant, blood filled with disease."

"Just don't give up," she pleaded, bending toward him, grabbing his hand, trembling.

"I'm not giving up. I'll never give up," he said, returning to a frenzy of tears.

"You won't die," I said, wanting to give him confidence, trying to close the possibility of his death even to myself. I didn't want to look at it. "You're too strong, too determined." My words lacked force of conviction, betraying my own uncertainty. I was far from sure that he would live and it frightened me. We both knew that I was uttering wishful lies.

"I hope you're right," he said. "It's a terrible way to die. I've seen people shivering their last days under heaps of blankets. I've seen them turn terrible shades of yellow because the treatment destroyed their livers. When the chemo kills your immune system, you're really vulnerable. One man had to have his groin excised to remove the uncontrollable jock itch fungal infection. He died a couple weeks later because they didn't get it all. Imagine dying of jock itch. Pneumonia gets a lot of us, drowning while lying in bed. Any bacteria can eat you alive. I got to know one guy my age, a fungus grew in his sinuses and ate into his brain. It's all so ugly."

"I cannot imagine having to face that," I said.

"I'll tell you what's worse," he said, choking up. "I feel like I brought this upon myself. I knew better. I went back to work at something I hated. I absolutely hated it. It was all-consuming. I lied about my dislike, I fell into a stupor. The damned money kept me there. Now I'm sick again. I feel like I sold my soul."

"But I hate my job everyday," I said, illustrating that I was not ill, trying to curb his unnecessary self-blame.

"I'm telling you, I forgot what was important. It went beyond my job. Discontent can cause a literal disease. Health and happiness are synonymous. Passion could have saved me. I lost my reverence. I stopped listening to my own sermons."

He sounded irrational to me. He was looking for reasons in the brutality of random events. He was shattered by fate and groping through the debris, trying to piece together shards that defied assembly. He was trying to link coincidence. He reduced his relapse to the wounds of his psyche, to forgetfulness and slipping. I had had enough science to know that he was grasping at air. I wanted him to stop heaping guilt onto his already overburdened soul.

"Daedalus knew why Icarus fell into a grave of watery hell," he said dramatically, like the poems that I used to listen to him reciting. I didn't know what he meant. I remembered his likening of poets to madmen.

"What?" I asked, frustrated by his cryptic verse, pained by his agony.

"I will not go gentle into that good night!" he grated out, pulsing like a fighter, incensed as a cornered animal, responding not to me, but upwards, as if addressing vague forces of control. He was so traumatized that he was in another dimension. I felt like he was beyond the aid of my friendship.

"Let it all out, my love," cried Jody, hating to see him rave, but seeming to believe that it was what he needed.

And he screamed and swore hellish abominations. He did not want to die. I had never seen rage so pure and unfiltered. His desire for life was absolute. His wailing passion, like an explosion, deafened the part of me that doubted emotional contributions to health. Given his will to live, in the magnitude of its expression, over that of someone who was indifferent to his own survival, how could any rational mind not give my friend the higher odds? At least that is what I told myself to get rid of the same deafening howl that was my own extreme fear of losing him.

His rage continued to pour for a few minutes and then, as if purged, as if he had no more tears to shed, his mood gave way to a calmer reflection. His storm had passed for the moment.

"Well," he said, still sullen, but with the hint of a smile, "That actually felt pretty good. Now what are we going to do?"

"Whatever you want, it's your day, my dear," said Jody.

"I've got what ... sixty some hours before I have to be locked in my cell? I can't just sit around here waiting for it to come. I've got to do something. My God, I can't believe I have to face this again." The sadness was starting to creep back in already. He could not escape his collision with the wall that was so fast approaching. There was no slowing down. He could only brace himself. He could only try to savor the time before impact. "I want to live. I want to go fly," he said. I wasn't sure what he had in mind, but we all left his apartment because he was a condemned man and he was calling the shots.

Living every day like it was your last was a fine mantra for anyone not dying. I didn't know if my friend was trying to squeeze excitement into his limited time or if he believed that elation could help save him. I realized that he actually wanted to fly when we pulled into the tiny municipal airport, next to a lonely office building and a ramshackle hanger. He made literal interpretations of his figurative yearnings. After brief arrangements, we crowded into a four person plane, Jody and I in the back, the pilot and my friend in the front. Whatever the reason, he burned for a few moments of escape. He couldn't just sit at home. He lusted for an eagle's freedom. Our take-off hinted of exhilaration, but lacked the release, the unfettered thrill. Circumstance allowed no euphoria.

As we lifted into the air the melancholy flew with us. The more that he yearned to be free of despair, the more depressing seemed the futility. Flight could not raise us above our burden; it was everywhere. The view was spectacular but tainted. We looked upon the rolling hills colored with the pastels of autumn like a painting that was singed on the periphery. These were visions that he would be smuggling into his hospital room, images that he would conjure as he laid weak with nausea. He loved the meandering brooks, he loved the beaver ponds and the hardwood forests. He wanted to take it all in, he wanted to absorb it, he wanted to feel it. A tear streaked his face. The more he loved it, the more he feared its being taken away. His eyes were witness to the cruel summary of all that he adored. It was a taunting last indulgence for his senses.

We flew over the house where he had grown up. He said that he wished that his parents had never sold it and lamented that nothing lasts forever. He pointed toward the apple orchard and the yard where he used to play, to that parcel of land that had been the theater of his life, where he acted out his diversions and follies, his dreams and strivings. It was a torturous vantage point, a God's-eye view, a final survey of his history, filled with doubt and longing.

He was in agony. The sweetness of joys past and present shook his soul. I wondered if he thought about jumping out of the plane, just to get it over with. He was wrenched, but he kept watching intently. As he sat next to the pilot crying, next to a man he didn't know, I realized the extent of what my friend had already overcome.

After the plane landed, it was time for dinner and we drove to his favorite restaurant. The news of his relapse had already spread throughout the small town in which he lived and the moment we entered the building he was greeted by the proprietor with open arms and sympathy that poured without restraint. Goodness radiated in her eyes. In addition to the promise of her thoughts and prayers, she offered dinner on the house. As we walked to our table, other townspeople turned from their meals in order to express their regrets. My friend deeply appreciated this collective kindness. One woman approached him and reached into her purse and handed him a piece of amethyst. Then, while rubbing his back, said that it had always brought her good luck. I was affected greatly by these acts of compassion. They were of obvious benefit to my friend's spirit. They were clear indications that people cared, that he was bound by community. Yet their words of empathy and understanding made me consider my own effectiveness.

The unfolding of circumstances lent to a rare evening of self-illumination. I was keenly aware of my trial and, as every second passed, vividly conscious of my failure. I was sitting directly across from my friend, during a dinner in which I had every opportunity for openness and honest reflection. My heart yearned to express its sentiments, but I was trapped inside a bubble of my own, encased within discomfort and vulnerability. This was no regular meal. It echoed of a last supper. In the extremity of the situation, I got a painful glimpse at my own psychology. I struggled with conversation. I saw my own reality, that I was more at ease chipping at rocks, caressing the inanimate, than I was with the tender aspects of humanity. I strayed from anything meaningful. My own feelings were beyond my ability to communicate. I couldn't tell him that I was afraid of losing him, that I would miss his laughter, that I would miss his good cheer. I couldn't vocalize what his friendship meant to me or how much I appreciated him. I repeatedly put my foot in my mouth. In my search for conversation I asked Jody if she had any plans for the near future, knowing full well that she would be with him every hour of every day. I asked my friend what he intended to do when he was released from the hospital, turning away from the possibility of his death with fabricated confidence. Sadly, my emotional reticence blocked a deeper connection between us. Like a closed door I was more secure when bolted shut. Uttering "love" was an impossibility. Love in its exposure could be gnawed by things darkly predatory. My disease was an inability to express myself. I clung to the safety of shared recollections. The evening progressed with him trying to savor every last bite of his meal while I interjected nothing more than trivia.

When we arrived back at his apartment it was still relatively early, but he wanted to go to bed. I think he wanted to spend some time alone with Jody. She was a beautiful young woman. She listened to him and sat confidently in the thickness of sorrow even when the atmosphere turned to grim silence. Compassion radiated in her glance. She was a loving participant, she had a role, she would be nowhere but by his side. I listened to them upstairs exchanging muffled whimperings and sweet-nothings. They were afraid of being parted. He gave her as much assuring affection as she gave him. Even though it was his life that was threatened, he knew that she too needed solace. I lay on the couch petting the dog, thinking of my bungled offerings, wondering what he saw in me as a friend, wishing that I had someone to console me for my inadequacies.

I awoke on Saturday dreading the new day, wondering how we would fill the time. When my friend came downstairs he appeared somewhat refreshed, as if sleep had partly rejuvenated his strength, but he seemed in his own world, and he said very few words to me. He obviously had a lot on his mind, issues that every person must sort for himself when grave moments arrive, but I couldn't help wondering if he was disappointed in me. I wanted to be of assistance, to help him, but didn't want to disturb his reflections if that was what he needed. I wondered what thoughts coursed through his head. He had to be confronting his hospitalization. He must have meditated on getting through the pricks and incisions of surgery, overcoming the nausea and the constant intrusions. He knew that his entire body would atrophy, that his muscular physique would deteriorate into a series of protruding bones, that his vivacity would ooze from him in the form of vomit and diarrhea. I considered the trial of preparing oneself for such conditions. He had a lot to think about. He was making breakfast, not in a bad mood, not with elation, but almost hypnotized. When he walked through those hospital doors he wanted to be confident, ready to face the horrors of his treatment but assured that they would be temporary, that he would survive. While he was imprisoned inside an enfeebled body and four sterile walls he had to somehow keep his equanimity. It seemed sadistic, like a torture so universally immoral as to be outlawed during war. Yet he had to walk in upright, facing it, and even sign the consent forms.

He prepared a very large breakfast. He wanted to get as much nourishment as he possibly could. He placed a plate on the table for me and then took a tray up to Jody, who was still in bed. After he finished his breakfast he made two eggs for the dog, leaning down and kissing her head while she ate, rubbing her soft white fur, saying, "Yes, I love you, sweet Siska, I love you, sweet baby." I felt a sad rush of sentimentality. He made me remember my old dog, how sad I was when we had to put her to sleep.

After several minutes he called upstairs to Jody, "Honey, are you ready to go? There's lots that I want to see today. There are colored autumn trees, pumpkin patches, wild apples, children diving in leaf piles, brown corn stalks ornamenting front yards."

Jody came down quickly and kept her face hidden from my friend by pretending to be looking for something. I caught a glimpse of her. She had been crying. "Yeah, I'm ready," she said in a slightly quaking voice.

"All right. We're off to seize another beautiful day," he said. And we left his apartment, taking the dog with us. He was in possession of a calm rapture, hovering for the moment above the muck of his reality.

He wanted to go hiking in the woods. As his time was winding down, he wanted to savor what was most precious to him. We drove to an isolated area of state forest that he knew well, a place that obviously had very few visitors, if any at all. He grabbed his hiking stick from the back of the truck and led Jody and me down a stream bed that he knew. He looked like the quintessential woodsman, his large frame donned in plaid, hiking stick finding placement with calculation, white dog bounding by his side. He appeared a vision of health. No onlooker would know that he was filled with villainous malignancies. It didn't make sense. I was out of breath lagging behind him and he was two days away from chemotherapy.

His condition eluded reason. One of life's cold irrefutable truths then swept me like chill air down the back of my neck: life was unfair. It didn't matter if you kept in shape or wore your seat belt or said your rosary every night. You could be plucked from the masses at any moment, unwillingly and at random. Life is just a game of Russian roulette and we play it every day whether we like it or not. My friend continued to walk down the path, pointing out trees and rock formations of particular beauty. He said that he and Jody had been looking for a piece of wooded property like this to build a little house upon. His disease was also the abortion of his dreams. He bent down and smelled an autumn flower and then, after a few steps, reached into an apple tree and picked a misshapen apple, imperfect in its wildness. He took a bite and said that it was bitter but delicious. There were laid stone walls covered with thick moss and he wondered if the land was once a yard that was now overgrown.

There was a rustling in the crisp fallen leaves. The dog bolted ahead and we speculated that the noise might have been caused by a deer. We broke into a jog, hoping to see wildlife. Then a shrill piercing scream rang throughout the forest, a hideous high-pitched cry that echoed with pain and fear, not unlike a child in terror. The dog had a raccoon in her jaws and she was shaking it back and forth frantically like a frenzied shark. The raccoon, powerless in the grip of such force, looked like a limp cloth doll being mercilessly ravaged, each savage twist of the dog's head embedding fangs deeper into tender flesh. It was an all-too-vivid view of a terrible way to die. I never knew that an animal's scream could sound so human.

Life was unfair to all living things. My friend cried out for the dog to stop. The dog paused and the raccoon, hanging flaccidly, slowly bent its head upward as if to glimpse its assailant, confused with fear, to attempt a feeble retaliatory bite, and the dog, seeing the raccoon still alive, continued the brutal wringing amid more dreadful cries. My friend shouted, "SISKA, NO!," as he hurled his hiking stick at the dog, wailing her in the hindquarters, delivering injury, and the dog, confused and betrayed, ran with her treasure into the distance. My friend cried hysterically as though he had come unwound, "I'm sorry, Siska ... you didn't know!" He had thrown his stick because he had wanted it all to stop. But he had hurt the dog. He hated being the creator of cruelty because he knew what it felt like. He also knew the screams of the raccoon. Those screams had entered his ears and mingled with his own. "Why?" he cried as he turned in slow circles with his head arched toward the sky, "Why?" He stumbled drunkenly in bewilderment and then fell to the ground in a heap like a puppet whose strings had all been snipped. Tears streaked the his face and he bellowed, "Why does it have to hurt so much?!"

Why did I just stand there like a stupefied stranger, like an unfeeling dimwit with my hands in my pockets, counting the hours before I could go home?

Jody ran over to him with tears rolling off her cheeks. He stood up, still hysterical, still enraged, and began unbuttoning his shirt, staggering under the burdens upon his mind. He took it off and threw it with indiscretion. He removed his T-shirt and did the same. It was cold. I could see his breath. I could see the scars on his chest from his former surgeries. He exposed his skin to the chill air because it was a reflexive semi-conscious statement of endurance, a primal display of brawn in preparation for the fight, revealing his character, his emotional rawness, his lunatic lust for the romantic. He picked up Jody in his arms, cradling her the way one would carry the wounded. They kissed, their lips wetted with the salt of each other's tears. Then he ran with her as if he just wanted to carry them both away. The muscles in his back rippled with strength, the same muscles that would soon begin their atrophication. This was a moment of intense fear and love. He stopped running and recited the last stanza of a poem to her:

> *If life ever deems that I lose thee*
> *I will defy this cruel decree*
> *And I will meet you in the swirling light of dawn*
> *On the shore, where the land meets the sea.*

In that moment, in each other's arms, they were on fire. They were both keenly alive. Life flowed through them deliberately and with precision. They wanted fiercely to remain that way. They were charged with vibrance and vitality. I felt like I was the only one dying.

That night, after we had found the dog and left the woods, they just wanted to be alone, to be away from me, and I understood that. And on Sunday morning, after my friend came down stairs and said that he had had a nightmare in which no one could recognize his disfigured corpse at his own wake, I had to leave; it was all that I could take. I fumbled through excuses about having to catch up on work and do my laundry. He knew that I was crumbling. He knew that his tortures would be difficult for anyone to witness. I hope he was aware that my distress and discomfort resulted only because of how deeply I cared.

I am back at work now, at this job that deadens my senses. It is

Thursday. I am still overwhelmed. He has been receiving chemotherapy for four days and I don't know how he is doing. I am afraid to call. I am afraid of bad news. I don't want to hear that he is throwing up or going out of his mind. Instead, I am numbly watching the arm of the backhoe dig scoop after scoop while I wonder why I didn't even cry. He probably wanted a friend to cry with him. What more tragedy could there have been? What would it have taken for me to shed a tear? He once taught me about mythology, about gazing into that which is so hideous that one turns to solid rock. I feel as though I am cracking. I have been gazing into the ugliness of life, I have been staring at Medusa. I am frozen. I am petrified. I am stone.

∞

6   The ICU

This story was written by Josh in the voice of his fiancée as she watches the man she loves lie near death. It is an incomplete chapter for time was the enemy; Josh's mind was not clear and his literary skills were diminished as death inched closer.

There was a change in everyone's mindset when they sent him to the ICU. A deeper fear arrived like a ghoulish intrusion as the odds of his survival dropped a few more notches. Hope dimmed like the bricking-up of windows and the closing of doors, as if exits were being sealed, limiting options, furthering confinement. The move to the ICU confirmed our suspicions that his health was slipping from bad to worse. We had felt his temperature rising, seen the distention in his abdomen and we knew that it wasn't good, but when they said ICU it was still devastating. I wanted to fight against it, I wanted to take him home and make him chicken soup and dab his forehead with water and give him love until he was better. The ICU had life support systems, blinking monitors that told the tale of one's rising and falling. It was a symbol of instability, a place where lives hung in the balance. When they brought the gurney, my eyelids filled and then spilled over. He looked so helpless as he was transferred from his bed, damp with sweat, to the railed gurney platform, his eyes beginning to hint of vacancy. He didn't know what was going on. The drugs and fever were loosening his hold on reality. To the late-shift attendants packaging him in sheets, he was just another unlucky cancer patient going to the fourth floor.

They went through the motions of gentleness, but their actions were the choreography of routine. They saw this everyday. People got sick and died. It wasn't pretty, but it happened. They distanced themselves from patients this ill. Their flat-lined detachment contributed to my emotional unraveling. Every shortage of concern or lip-service to kindness fueled my hostility. He deserved the best, he loved life, he was a fighter. I should have been the one tucking the sheets around him, his mother and I would have been more gentle, his father would have lifted him more tenderly than anyone on the hospital staff. Affection could be like tiny doses of medicine, love like little pills. Every bit helped when things got this serious. No bad thoughts, only love and prayers. "I didn't do anything, I'm innocent," he cried as they wheeled him away. Neither one of us deserved this. It was agonizing to watch him slip. His health was so bad that he needed protection that went far beyond the cradling of my arms around him. I tried to calm myself. He needed some intensive care, just for a little while. Ultimately he would be all right. With silent repetitions I told myself he was going to be all right.

The atmosphere on the fourth floor was hurried, with undertones of panic, as if our arrival was compounding a crisis already in progress. The medical staff was congested around a doorway on the opposite side of the nurses' station, orders were dictated and supplies were quickly gathered and shuttled into the room. Failing health demanded immediate action. The attendants wheeled my love into his new room and handed his heaping medical chart to a nurse that followed us in. The room smacked me with its bleakness and sterility. The nurse stated that she had expected our arrival, that they were having a rough night. My love was transferred to his new bed. He was perspiring and restless, he sat up even though he was weak and then demanded with all his rage for someone to bring him a "five dollar soda." His mind swirled with unconscious interpretations of his frightful reality. He must have been thirsty. The nurse forcibly tried to get him to lie down, she told us that his orders called for him to be on oxygen immediately. She wanted him to lie back and relax, but was having no luck. He was unruly and irrational. He grimaced with spite like an angry child and struggled against the nurse's grasp. The nurse turned to his father for help, hoping that he could coax him.

"Lie down and rest, everything is going to be all right," his father said, stroking his shoulders, trying to pacify him.

He squirmed against the restraint, calling out in anger, "Where's Mom? You promised me she would be here! Where is she?" His mother was crying in the hall, out of his line of vision. She was getting ready to retire to the hospitality house for the night. She had all that she could take. "You promised you would get us out of here!" He continued to fight. He batted the oxygen mask from the nurse's hand, fearfully crying that he wouldn't allow an "octopus" to be put on his face. This was the man who had swept me off my feet with his kindness and charm. I ached as I watched his mental disassembly. Incrementally from the day of our first date his face had come to represent the perfect combination of features and form, and whether glowing with happiness or distorted with rage, I loved him. I silently encouraged his fight. He swatted at the nurse, pleading to be set free. I could see that, at the very least, his determination was intact. Each swipe of anger and every unintelligible cry of insult assured me that he was not ready to succumb to anything.

"I'm going to give him a sedative," the nurse exclaimed in frustration.

I didn't want to see him knocked out, but he was completely unmanageable and I didn't want him to get hurt in the struggle. It took a double dose before he finally calmed down. Even then he strangely avoided sleep, hovering in blank consciousness as though he had been lobotomized, like a container void of contents. His empty expression mocked the intelligence and wit that I had come to love. I almost expected a sudden "Boo!" accompanied by a jerkish motion and a laugh, underscoring his playfulness. I wanted it to be a joke. This reality didn't seem possible. No wild constructions of my imagination could have prepared me for this ghastly scenario. Yet the unimaginable had presented itself. He looked like he had been in a car accident. He was limp with injury. He had been smashed between a relentless disease and a reckless treatment. His body struggled to keep its most basic systems functioning. Dripping fluids supplemented his hold on life, providing the balm for his internal wounds. His skin was blotched with the tiny bruises of bursting capillaries. He panted for want of oxygen underneath the muffling plastic mask. I had to get through this. These were just the first five minutes of the ICU. I wanted to rip each of us from this horrible backdrop and paste us in a new place and time.

I had learned enough about medicine to be frightened for his life, but was layman enough to retain my faith in his convalescence. The bad news was that he had just entered a period of extreme vulnerability that could last for several weeks. The chemotherapy, in destroying his leukemic cells, also destroyed a great deal of his healthy cells, including those of his digestive tract, his hair follicles, and his bone marrow. The worst news of all was that his immune system was wiped out. He had no defenses against even the mildest of contagions. This was the reason that he had a fever. He had caught something. These infections were frequently devastating. Pinpointing the responsible bacteria, fungus, or virus was a difficult task, and so, to provide the only defense possible, the doctors put him on antibiotics, which only worked on certain bacteria and the occasional fungus, bypassing viruses altogether. But antibiotics, in their imperfection, did damage of their own to already overtaxed organs. The best scenario called for the rapid return of his own immune system, but his white blood cell count was still dropping, and its recovery was a long way off. A normal immune system had a white count of anywhere from 3,500 to 10,000 cells per cubic centimeter. His was two hundred and falling. He had to make it through a prolonged period of excessive fragility. And there were other complications. I wished I never had to have this medical education. These were facts I could have happily lived without. There was no good news.

The doctor came into the room, peering into charts. He greeted us apathetically and already I didn't like him. He seemed as drab and lackluster as the hospital walls; he was not one of the regular physicians that we were accustomed to seeing. He was a stranger who we never had the opportunity to scrutinize, perhaps demoted to the night-shift for a reason. In this man with unfamiliar credentials and flaccid impact we were asked to place our trust. You never knew what kind of doctor you were going to get. Some were wonderfully caring, some were cold, some you just hated. You chose the ones you liked when you could, and you hid your dislike of the callous or indifferent ones who were sent your way. You bit your tongue when you were mad because you needed something from every one of them. The doctor began his examination, shining a light into my love's eyes and then pressing on his swollen abdomen and listening to places on his torso with a stethoscope. His brief inspection seemed to confirm his expectations. He sighed inauspiciously, looking grim and in thought, as if pondering verbal maneuvering. "Well," he said, "I'm afraid that he's not good. His temperature is 104 degrees, he definitely has some kind of infection. We're running tests now to try to figure out what it is. For the moment we've got him on broad range antibiotics that will cover most of the bacteria we normally see in this environment. I'm very concerned, however, with that distended abdomen. When was the last time that he had a bowel movement or passed gas?" The doctor's eyes directed the question to my love's father, who had the look of authority, the command of being male with the tie to the male doctor that went with it. But my love's father, lacking a detailed experience of the past few days, turned to me for the answer.

"Probably ... three days ago," I said. "He had a little diarrhea, but he hasn't eaten anything in a week either."

"Right," the doctor said. "But normally I would hear rumbling sounds indicating that there was activity, that peristalsis was taking place, even if there was no food substance to be moved. I'm afraid his digestive tract has ceased to function. There's no movement at all. We see this occasionally with highly ablative chemotherapy protocols. The distention is the result of his food actually ... breaking down, with nowhere to go, hence the bloating. It can be drained, partly, through a tube run down his nasal cavity and through his stomach. You should make sure that he doesn't have any kind of food or drink. He doesn't need anything else to contend with in those intestines. He'll receive all his fluids and nutrition intravenously." He paused, preparing to deliver another blow, then continued, "I'm afraid a draining tube might also have to be installed in his lungs. When he breathes I can hear fluid gurgling. This means that he might have pneumonia, which might, in fact, be the cause of his fever, but we'll know better tomorrow. I have to add that his liver and kidney function tests show that those organs are not performing well, in fact, they show a highly diminished capacity. His chart says that last year he had a bone marrow transplant. All the radiation and chemo of a transplant takes a toll on these organs. And now this new cycle of chemo. There's only so much a body can take after a while."

My love's father, overcome with disturbances, tried to retain his cohesion by reverting to his trademark assertiveness and we-can-make-it-happen optimism. He wanted to know the answer to the question that mattered most, but could only bring himself to ask, "These problems can all be overcome, right, Doc? We're still moving in a positive direction here. We're gonna' make this boy of mine better yet, aren't we?" His proud deep voice quaked with tremors.

"Let's just see how it goes," the doctor answered sullenly. "I'm sorry that I can't be any more help." And the doctor left us overwhelmed, sitting in front of a very sick young man that we loved, whose only sign of life was his chest filling and deflating in hurried repetitions.

I had known about his health problems even before we had

started dating. We were from the same small town, where tragic personal stories could not avoid circulation. I had known of his leukemia, of his bone marrow transplant, of his grandfather's death (the town mayor) only weeks after the transplant was completed, compounding his already poignant tale. He had recovered quickly, and on the occasions when I saw him walking down the street, he looked happy and robust. His hair was growing back in and it looked soft and thick like a puppy's, like it would be pleasant to the touch. He had a gleam in his eye that was wonderfully lively. A small town is like a world of its own and there was something about him that seemed very heroic. Mine was simply an attraction of passing until we were formally introduced several months later at the party of a mutual friend. We seemed to find conversation easily, he was as exciting as I had anticipated, delightfully different, and it felt like ignition, a trilling fiery beginning. I imagine that ours was a common start, the way love begins for any couple, catered to each other's interests and needs, hinting of predestination. He cautioned me on our second date that his disease could return in spite of all his treatments, in spite of how healthy he looked. It was a risk that I was willing to take, barely a consideration at all.

Leaving him on that first night in the ICU was an ordeal in itself. During his first ten days in the hospital I had slept right by his side on a small bed that could be packed away during the daytime hours. This was comforting for each of us, and he woke me frequently because he often needed his vomit basin emptied or a drink of soda or his sheets changed because of his diarrhea. I gave him the attention that the nurses could not provide. In little ways we could continue our romance. We could hold hands during the calm evening hours after all his visitors had left and the activity quieted in the hall. Those were precious nights, we could be alone and talk intimately about the stresses on our minds, we could watch a movie or share a laugh about certain quirky members of the hospital staff. The nights had become our time together. They were our attempt at regaining a semblance of normalcy in the midst of extremely abnormal conditions. Regulations didn't allow the same convenience in the ICU. Someone could stay with him overnight on a chair, but no beds were permitted because they could get in the way during an emergency. And now that his condition had grown so serious, other interests were moving in.

"Jody," his father said as he jostled me, waking me up. I had fallen asleep while leaning over on a pillow that I had placed by my love's side. His words seemed like the hazy continuance of a bad dream. "I want you to go stay with his mother in the hospitality house. Go get some real sleep. I've been thinking the best way to take care of him is in shifts. We'll have to organize a schedule of care giving. I'll take nights, I'm good at staying up late. His sister will be back tomorrow and she'll want to help. His aunt will be here too. This will have to be done logistically if we're going to get through it. You can come back in the morning after you've rested."

I was not accustomed to being told what to do, especially when it concerned issues so intimately personal. The affairs of my heart were my own. As the demands of his words nestled in, I began to feel the violation, but turned from my anger as it was hatching because our patient had woken up and required my attention. He tried feebly to sit up in bed. I could see that he needed something. Even though he was confused his face still conveyed signals of expression, slight muscular tuggings that were to me like a language. I knew what he wanted. His chin withdrew and his Adam's apple rose, on each side of his nose the skin raised like a snarl and his eyes squinted, extending tiny wrinkles like cracks creeping through glass.

"DO YOU HAVE TO THROW UP? DO YOU WANT SOMETHING TO DRINK? I WOULD GIVE YOU SOMETHING TO DRINK BUT YOU ARE NOT ALLOWED TO HAVE ANYTHING," his father said loudly, as if increased decibels could penetrate my love's incomprehension.

"He has to spit," I said, holding a pink basin up to his mouth, receiving a wad of phlegm. I raised the edge of the basin so as to wipe his lip of the trail that followed from his mouth. He had been grimacing peculiarly when he had to spit because his throat had been sore. Having to vomit would have brought a different set of facial hieroglyphics, as wanting a drink would have, or being in pain, or frustration, or being fed up with all the crap that he had to endure. I could read his distresses and longings the way a mother could read her infant child. This practiced attentiveness to a multitude of details composed a woman's sense of intuition. Any attempts by his father to make similar interpretations would be clumsy and potentially damaging.

His father gave orders indiscriminately like the captain of a sinking ship, trying to bring an order and command of others when it wasn't needed, when the best thing for everyone else was just to wallow in varying forms of self-expression. The intensity of his love ironically fueled a damaging behavior, it gave rise to a mania that was underlyingly frantic and jittery, which to conceal required excessive amounts of domination and assertion, the only methods of success that he knew. Hands that were too big for caressing, that did damage of their own when they merely were trying to provide care. To keep himself glued together he needed to embrace an element of control that could halt his plummet into the mind-splitting despair that was the uncontrollability of his son's life slipping through his fingers. In his pain and desire, in his indomitability, he was five times the size of a normal man. He hovered over his son, his huge frame hunched on a little chair. He took up the whole room.

"Why don't you go now, Jody. You'll need your rest if you want to take the day shift," his father said to me, still trying to commandeer the situation by implanting his idea of scheduling. I could have received sufficient rest in a series of interrupted cat naps. That was how the first ten nights in the hospital had passed. I had already lived it. Yet I gave in easily to his request, my will bending in the fogginess of late-night fatigue, feeling the meekness of my pliable resolve. I talked myself into the sensibility of his father's arguments, and in the self-rejection of conceding, I began to question my own role. I was not a family member. My title was merely girlfriend and I was weary of crossing boundary lines that marked the rights of relatives. There was a tacit doctrine that gave family the privilege of making decisions because they knew what was best for the patient. I deferred to his father's wishes even though I was the one closest to his son, even though I felt more like a wife than a girlfriend. I had given up my job to be there twenty-four hours a day. His father had made a habit of visiting only at dinner time. I had been the one wiping-up the vomit after midnight, caressing my love's cheek and whispering comfort. The details of care-giving eluded his father's mind, as he was moved only by great urgencies and industrial-sized complications, and now he wanted to take control of the inherently unmanageable situation like the company president that he was, with dictates and regimentation. I left for the night, but my displacement brought sorrow like the weeping of a mute little girl. As I walked out of the hospital into the darkness, my mind raced with a thousand grim possibilities of what could go wrong in my absence, that I might not have the opportunity to say good-bye to my sweet prince. The poorly lit sidewalk was lonely and frightening, my usual escort I had just left incognizant and feverish, hooked to dripping fluids, needing me.

* * *

The kind young intern named Steve lubricated his finger with gelled anesthetic and crammed into my love's right nostril, hoping to get the job done quickly, and my love, not understanding that this was a medical situation, squirmed and screamed with indignation, fighting against the inconceivability of our restraint, wickedly defiled, as though in his world a stranger had approached him on the street and forced two-thirds of a chubby finger up his nose. For him the incredible obscenity of this violation was an outrage and he flailed accordingly. Steve snaked the tube in, but when it hit the back of my love's throat he gagged and then retched, then Steve had to withdraw the tube and the whole hellish process had to be started all over again. To restrain someone you love is a heart-wrenching task. By its nature it goes against their wishes. I felt the discomfort of abetting in a crime; I had to keep reminding myself that this was for his good. His mother's expressions indicated that she felt the foul unpleasantness of it. Pinning him down ran contrary to her protective instincts. I was surprised by how easily I could hold back his left arm to keep him from grabbing the tube or striking Steve in the face. My love had been so strong. These were the same arms that had once held me so tightly, that picked me up and twirled me through the air to the music of my laughter. I could see that he was baffled by his own weakness. He had expected all of his former strength to be available for his defense, but this newfound absence of brawn seemed to aggravate his confusion. It belied his expectations like waking up to the shock of amputation, like missing a hand or a leg, being robbed of physical features that one fully expected to be in possession of.

Once the tube was in place he seemed to forget completely about it, his rage dissipated like smoke into the air, he harbored no residual anger and strangely drifted back into the calmness of his mental Neverland, replete with its odd decipherings. He hadn't had anything to drink in eighteen hours and his lips were developing areas of discoloration and peeling. He still had a bad fever. "Hello," he said, trying to get our attention in a voice that was now somewhat nasal from the implanted tube. "I'd like to order a freezy milk shake and a bubbler of water, please."

At that moment his sister Julie knocked and walked tentatively into the room and in the distraction of her presence his request went unacknowledged. Julie had been with us in the hospital for the first two days, but her job had drawn her away and she yielded to providing her support over the phone. Now that her brother was in the ICU she would remain indefinitely.

Steve the intern was puttering in the corner with the pumping mechanism. The focus of activity continued to be Julie's newfound presence, I was very glad to see her, and she received lavish embraces from her mother and me, the severity of the situation opening faucets of sorrow and tenderness. But Julie was unlike many women. She was not an easy recipient or purveyor of affection. Her first line of defense was an enigmatic wall that she used to keep out emotion, buttressed by a stubbornness that she inherited from her father, yet this likeness to him she denied feverishly, keeping old abuses interred. But the hospital setting forced confrontations. She would have to see her father later; he was away sleeping, preparing for the "night shift." Julie brought into the room a lot of intangible baggage, yet the scars that hid her wounds created an endearing irrepressibility. She was tough. She could tell you to shove it where the sun didn't shine. There was usually truth in her unequivocal assessments, and her unwavering confidence in her brother's recovery helped cleanse the mood of depression and negativity. Her distance from grief and sorrow allowed a much needed sense of humor to penetrate the bleak walls of the ICU. I felt a bond to Julie as a friend and an ally because to her there was simply no way that her brother was going to die.

"Give your brother a hug, dear, he loves you," his mother said to Julie as she wiped the tears from her eyes.

"Yeah, yeah. Hey, Bro," she said in an enough-of-this-emotion-crap tone before gazing down intently at his haggard face. "Man, you really look like shit. It's amazing what you do to get Mom and Dad's attention," she added, unaware that his intelligence was on vacation. She had been raised in his shadow, and had been stunted by the lack of light. She was only letting herself be hugged now because circumstances were extreme. She showed little grief or sorrow.

"I would really like to order a freezy milk shake and a bubbler of water, please, PLUS a barbecue pie," he said with careful enunciation, so as not to be misunderstood.

"What the hell? They turned him into a retard," Julie said, starting to chuckle. "Where does he think he is, a five star restaurant in Candyland?"

That was the first time I had laughed in days. She offered the same type laughter that my love did. He and his sister had the same sense of humor. He would have been the first one to poke fun at his own nonsense. I trusted her brazen confidence in her brother's recovery. She had witnessed a lifetime of his triumphs, she knew him the way only a sibling could.

"He'll be fine, quit your worrying. You're gonna' be fine, aren't you, chickenhead?" Julie continued, now to herself. "When we were teenagers sneaking beer, who got caught? I did. He was my other half. There would be a void like a black pit without him, my world would fall away. My heart would feel the exile of loneliness. I thought of the days when I could have been kinder. My mind made an uncontrollable hideous leap to a tombstone, to a cruel parting, to an ending. "

"He's very sick, dear. You shouldn't make fun of him," their mother retorted with a wishy-washy reprimand, torn between the benefits of levity and the desire to defend her injured child. Impotent in her reprimand, her finger wagged a lovably ineffective "tsk-tsk."

Just then Steve flipped the switch that began the pumping process. Accompanying a rhythmic hum came a procession of brown liquid waste that crawled between interspersions of air bubbles in the clear tubing that ran from my love's nostril to a receiving vessel. The viewing of this foulness was a force that drew us back toward fear, toward revulsion and the sorrow of his reality. My love looked down stupidly with cross-eyed befuddlement at the train of brown sludge that marched from his nose and away from the cesspool that his intestines had become. He was blissfully oblivious to the precariousness of his own life. "I had a dream about kicking your ass," he said to the intern that was responsible for the implantation of the tubes down his nose and lungs.

The ICU was already causing emotions to fray and alliances to unfurl. The hysteria and stress and fatigue triggered undesirable disintegration. His mother's unwanted proximity to the domination of her ex-husband, with his array of behaviors dredged from a painful past. She was falling to pieces, yet my embrace merely stemmed from courtesy, my tears were strictly my own, for I needed all of my available energy to console myself.

What is it that makes one alive or dead? He still had the microscopic cellular exchanges, the organic conduits that were shipping routes for sustenance and waste. Confidence .... intuitive knowledge or denial, was there something that I wasn't looking at, was I naive and hopeful or did I just know him better? Confidence in the patient even when he is lost somewhere in the depths of lunacy ... presupposing that even in lunatic ramblings there is something of the life force that holds on, that knows, that wants to continue living. The little ways the life force manifests ... the trickery of the popsicle, the pulling the tube from the nose. Something about the medical staff and the medicine itself that is the enemy, certainly on the surface the motives are good, but something primal takes over when some agent is causing injury to one so loved (defense, protection). Medical wisdom ... doctors in expensive clothing and watches, what wisdom did they have, what knowledge other than the strict science, what cognizance of elements more human, of emotion, what right did they have to predict death, as if in the prediction it gave them more control in an arena where pompous minds couldn't admit fallibility? I thought, "They are not smart enough to make him better, so why should they be smart enough to know that he is going to die."

"Let's discharge him from the ICU. I'll get the paperwork." He had proved them all wrong. That was the way he was, that was my love. I was proud of him, there were monuments made upon my heart. He was going to be all right.

∞

7 Final Days

Following a fourteen-month remission after his bone marrow transplant, Josh relapsed and was in and out of several medical establishments over the next two-and-a-half years. In September, 1995 he opted to enter Bassett Hospital, Cooperstown, for further chemotherapy treatment where he spent eight hellish days in the ICU. The doctor assembled the family and related his worst fear—Josh would not make it through the night. But, he celebrated his twenty-seventh birthday in the ICU and was released in mid-November.

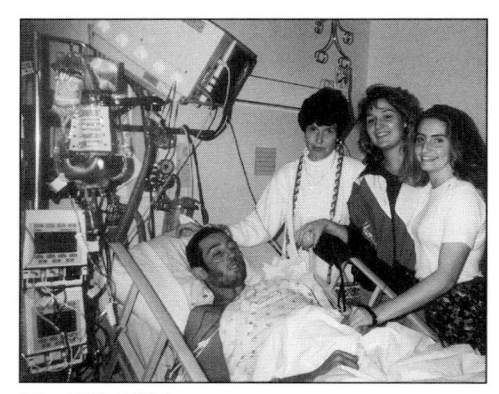

The ICU, 1995

Weak and barely able to walk after his release, he flew to Reno, Nevada with his father and Jody for a month-long, holistic treatment. After a brief trip East for the Christmas holiday, Josh and Jody returned to Reno in January, 1996 for continuing treatment. By late March, feeling rejuvenated, they returned to New York where they immediately packed their gear to begin a camping tour across the United States—final destination Alaska. They first turned south to Hilton Head with plans to continue on to the French Quarter in New Orleans, canoe the *Rio Grande* and explore the *Grand Canyon*.

On their visit to Hilton Head, we canoed Broad Creek, fighting what felt like hurricane force winds as we laughed and cursed our way down the "creek." Josh kept saying, "Paddle harder, Mom!" Stop paddling even for a second and the wind would blow us backward, and the "ground" we so valiantly struggled to gain would be lost. Oh, how my arms ached! A time I'll never forget.

Josh and Jody called frequently enroute regaling their travel escapades. In early May they headed for Reno where it was discovered he had relapsed once again. He was rushed to the hospital for emergency phoresis— a procedure that had to be repeated twice in order to remove the dangerously high blast cells. *(Note: Phoresis is a four-hour long process. Blood is removed through a tube inserted in one arm, passed through a specialized machine to separate the cancerous blast cells from the healthy ones, and ultimately returned to the patient through a tube in his other arm. This same process is also used to gather T-cells and platelets.)*

I immediately flew to Reno, joining my ex-husband Jim and his sister Judith, whose nursing experience comforted us as we flew via *Air-Med* back to Albany. Time was crucial. We were back full circle at the Albany Medical Center where once-optimistic doctors turned an unsympathetic ear and refused to attempt a recommended, experimental treatment.

We were offered no hope. Diagnosis: Death by summer's end.

Never one to give up, Jim began his search anew and found a doctor in Syracuse who was willing to try the innovative treatment. It was a gift of hope. On May 6, 1997 Josh entered Crouse Irving Memorial Hospital in Syracuse, New York. Reacting violently to the unproven treatment, he suffered congestive heart failure and developed a fungal infection in his lungs. He spent weeks in

Cardiac Intensive Care and ICU. Amazingly he recovered. Where he found the strength and determination, I'll never know. He was so focused on recovery! How could he not survive?

But by mid-August, after a three month confinement, there was nothing even our new team of doctors could do. With no words of encouragement or hope of survival, he was discharged into my care. I took my son home on the fifteenth of August. The hospital staff taught me to administer his antibiotics through his chest port. All his health care products and equipment were delivered directly to the house—oxygen, antibiotics and a wheelchair. The county nurse initially visited daily, monitoring my basic nursing skills, eventually limiting her visits to once a week in order to draw his blood for the dreaded CBC. Hospice was suggested but was never a consideration. For us, hospice meant death. And Josh was not going to die.

Each of us tried to proceed with our normal routine. In the privacy of his own home, Josh focused on recovery, allowing his body to heal from the unrelenting leukemic attack; Jody continued her studies and volleyball competition; Julie juggled her coaching career with her weekend trips home to visit her brother; and Jim struggled to balance the variant pressures of his son's illness, his business and his life with his second family. I was responsible for Josh's care—twenty-four hours a day, seven days a week. It was physically exhausting and emotionally stressful. I lived each day in utmost fear. I was terrified. I kept charts. I administered antibiotics. I dispensed vitamins. I cooked. I waited.

Miraculously, by mid-October Josh was making great progress. He gained weight and no longer needed twenty-four hour oxygen support. He could walk unassisted. Now was my chance to slip home for a few days to regroup, as I had been up north for six months. I left his care in the capable hands of my trusted friend, Carole. I shall forever be indebted to her for allowing me the opportunity to take a much needed break. I called daily to assure myself he was doing well, easing my guilt at abandoning him yet again. My plans were to return Thanksgiving week. They were soon thwarted. Josh called, hysterical and frightened, afraid that the swollen lymph nodes in his neck indicated the leukemia had returned once more.

Calming his fear took all my strength for I was as panicked and frightened as he was. My words were comforting. But deep down, neither of us believed them. My role had always been to soothe his fears while offering my motherly assurances. We clung to the hope that survival was inevitable. Experience re-enforced our belief that miracles can and do happen; besides, his cell counts were in the normal range. But, his pain steadily increased. This was a sign the disease continued to rage. I was desolate.

Packing to return was unendurable. As I placed my black dress into my suitcase, I hoped I wouldn't need it. My three-week reprieve in the tranquility of my home ended. When I saw Josh, it was clearly visible that he had lost weight in my absence. Guilt besieged me. I should have stayed. We could not afford even the slightest setback.

While I was gone, Josh, forever the optimist, bought Jody an engagement ring and on November 2, 1997 announced his engagement. The wedding date was set for July 25, 1998 at the Columbus Community Church. I remember his excitement. He was so happy and so proud of the beautiful diamond ring he had chosen. Since the majority of his time was spent in bed, he tucked the ring securely under his pillow, ready at hand to slip on Jody's finger as soon as she returned home from her volleyball game. She was thrilled! He was elated!

By Thanksgiving, Josh showed minor improvements. My sister Kathy and her family decided to make the 600 mile trip east for the holiday. On the surface all appeared normal. The delicious aroma of the roasting turkey permeated the air. The pumpkin pies were ready to be savored. We had a great time and I was grateful for their visit. I often wonder if Kathy knew this would be the last time she would see her nephew alive.

The fall days passed quickly as Christmas rapidly approached. We battled holiday crowds trolling the mall seeking those special, treasured gifts. As I pushed Josh in his wheelchair, he found untold delight in selecting the perfect presents. We had to finish quickly, though, as his strength began to fade.

Julie, Rodey, Josh, Jody—Christmas, 1997

With a roaring fire blazing and pine smells filling the air, Josh lay on the couch, laughing uproariously as Jody and I struggled with the fifteen-foot Christmas tree. After we had traipsed through the snow and spied the "perfect" tree in the stand of pines beside the house, we chopped it down, dragged it what seemed like miles, and finally managed to shove it through the door. Getting it upright was no small feat. It had seemed so much smaller outside, covered with snow. We decorated its majestic boughs with brightly colored lights and all the handmade decorations saved since their childhood. It was difficult to spot the tree among the mountain of brightly wrapped gifts.

Always the first to awaken, Christmas morning was no exception. I brewed the coffee and rekindled the smoldering embers in the fireplace while I waited for my children to roll out of bed. We spent the entire morning individually opening our gifts ... watching each other's reaction was always an added pleasure. We stopped only to refill our coffee cups. To top the morning off, I made the traditional Webb family breakfast—sausage, bacon, eggs and blueberry pancakes. Christmas was lavish—a Christmas I will always cherish!

Josh's last outing was a Sunday afternoon, December 28. Armed with a pocket full of Demerol and a bottle of water, we (Julie, Jody, Josh, and I) went to the movies to see the newly released *Titanic*. What an incredible love story! As we drove home, no one uttered a word. Our throats were thick, tears clouded our eyes as each was lost in private thoughts of young love, young lives tragically cut short. No one dared mention the parallel. During the funeral service, Becky, Josh's high school classmate, sang the movie's theme, "My Heart Will Go On." I am unable to hear that song without thinking of Josh.

Three days later on New Year's Eve, we raced frantically to the

Syracuse emergency room. Josh's pain had became intolerable and the narcotic skin patch that steadily delivered his pain medication was no longer effective. He needed a quicker and more effective way to get the demerol into his system. He needed an IV.

Friends and neighbors continued their visits, lending their loving support, including Tom and his very pregnant wife, Amy. Josh and Tom had been neighbors, camping pals and drinking buddies. Amy and Julie had been high school classmates. As Josh reverently touched Amy's child-swollen belly, he was able to feel the baby move beneath his ashen fingers.

Josh with Sophie

On January 29, Amy and Tom returned with a week-old Sophie in their arms. I gently laid Sophie on Josh's chest and he wept as he carefully cradled this precious new life. It was a bittersweet moment as I, too, cried for the child he would never father, his child he would never hold. Josh died two days later.

The house buzzed with activity on Friday, January 30th—Jim stopped by; Julie returned for the weekend; Scott, Josh's lawyer briefly stopped by with his revised will and Reverend Steve joined us.

As Josh lay relaxing on the couch, Jim massaged his swollen feet while we talked, laughed and reminisced. We spent a quiet evening around the fire enjoying the camaraderie and warmth of our reunited family.

Was it Kismet that we were all together that night? It was not planned. It just happened. How ironic to sign your will the night before you die.

Hands joined, heads bowed, Reverend Steve led us in prayer prior to his leaving. By ten o'clock that evening, Josh was physically exhausted and began experiencing some nausea. The relentless pain intensified, rendering the massive oral doses of Demerol ineffective. He began vomiting. He could not keep the medication in his system.

It was a vicious circle. He needed an IV which could only be administered at the hospital, but he wasn't ready to return. His pleas of "Mommy, Mommy, help me, help me!" shattered my broken heart. He reached for me. I tried to hug him tightly, but the slightest touch was painful, and physical contact was difficult. I was helpless once more. Nothing was effective. He was writhing in pain. Relief was not available.

It was a long, sleepless, terrifying night as I struggled with my choices. I called the hospital. I called the doctor. I paced the floor. I checked him constantly. I cried. Finally, in the early morning hours, I slipped quietly from their room, leaving Josh and Jody alone embracing, awaiting slumber and the dawn of a new day. We were always thankful for a new sunrise signaling another day of life. But this was to be our last. I didn't know death was only a few hours away. I was expecting another miracle.

I was dozing ... a brief, fretful nap when Jody startled me with her soft knock on the door. In the early hours of dawn, Josh finally admitted it was time to return to the hospital. Before he left, however, he wanted to distribute the remainder of his funds. He could barely sign his name.

Frantic, I made three phone calls that morning—the hospital, *911* and Jim. In the past, I had always taken Josh to the hospital or the doctor's office, but I automatically reached for the phone that morning to summon help. As I waited for the paramedics to arrive, I roamed the house like a caged tiger, crying, trying to be brave while I braced myself for the inevitable. As the team of six volunteer paramedics wheeled Josh to the waiting ambulance, he seemed calm, at peace with his decision to return. I know, without a doubt, he knew this was the end ... the battle was over. With so many details requiring my attention that morning, I had no time to be alone with him, no time for a private good-bye. How I hated the thought of returning to the hospital. It was a death sentence and a surrender to the battle we had fought so hard to win.

The flurry of activity accompanying our arrival at the hospital created waves of hysteria, of panic and of the horror yet to come. The doctors, the nurses and the arrival of family and friends did nothing to calm my frazzled nerves. I detested those preliminary hugs of comfort silently indicating death was at hand. As painful as it was, the time had come to let him go. His pain was insufferable. He could endure no more.

I will never forget the day he died ... it was Saturday—a bitterly cold day, the sunset looming on the horizon. My nephew Charlie was celebrating his twenty-first birthday. I was sitting at the foot of Josh's hospital bed, hugging Julie, crying and barely aware of the room filling with family and friends. Reverend Steve was saying a prayer as Josh gasped his last breath.

I don't remember leaving the hospital or driving back to Josh's house. I think Julie drove. I do remember, though, by the time we arrived, the house was filled with family and friends, and the aroma of their tangible offerings of sympathy infused the air. On the surface it seemed like a party in full swing. On closer examination, the grief and tears could be seen. People were everywhere, but the funeral arrangements awaited.

I was numb. There was so much to do. There was no time to grieve. It was Reverend Steve who prompted me to edit his preliminary obituary draft. Together we worked on the wording and then sought the input of family members. The planning of the funeral service was truly a family effort. We handled the multitude of details ... flowers ... music ... reception ... pallbearers ... seating arrangements ... calling hours ... a casket ... a burial plot. Where once there was strife, harmony prevailed. We were united as we planned our final tribute to a brave, young warrior.

Sometimes I wonder what else I could have done. Medical technology couldn't save him, so what could I have done? Self doubt and guilt crept into my mind. Loving accolades of comfort and support poured in—accolades I didn't feel were deserved or warranted. My place was always by his side, for I gathered strength from being close at hand. He was my child, where else would I be?

I remember how proud I felt when he was asked to appear on a segment of *Hard Copy* to recount his revolutionary treatment; how proud to see him featured on a local news broadcast honoring the unselfish men and women who heroically give the "gift of life" to others through their blood and plasma donations. How proud I was as he walked to the podium, he looked so handsome, so healthy as he stood before the camera. Emotion overcame him as he hugged one of his "blood brothers," thanking him for his precious gift.

I remember the terrifying images, as well. I am haunted by the fear in his voice during his initial phone call; haunted by the atrocities he endured over the years in the search for a cure; haunted by his cries of help; haunted as he cradled a week-old Sophie and wept; haunted by how cold he felt as I kissed him good-bye; and haunted by his image as he lay in the oak casket with the canoe paddle he had lovingly crafted for his father tucked at his side.

Months later, I received these cherished words of comfort from Reverend Steve:

Josh was one of the most unique persons I've encountered in my ministry. He taught me how to deal with the most crucial moments in the journey of life and smile and walk on. What a reward to have a son say, "My mom is an angel." Undoubtedly, you were the greatest assurance unto Josh that the sun would appear no matter how dark it became. Through his life many lives will not be the same, and I'm part of that number.

There will be no new moments of joy to capture on film ... no wedding to attend ... no grandchildren to hold ... no birthdays to celebrate ... no Christmases to share. Memories must sustain me.

Death is a cruel teacher, a painful way to learn, to set priorities. Each time I see a full moon, Josh is with me enhancing its value. Each time I see a canoe I think of Josh yelling, "Paddle harder, Mom!" Each time I see a sunrise I know a new day has begun and

Josh is with me.

It was my destiny and my privilege to be his mother and I will cherish forever the joy he brought to my life.

∞

EPILOGUE: *Hero's Farewell*

The funeral was incredible ... a day of tears, a day of laughter. On a cold and snowy February day, we buried Josh in the West Hill Cemetery, Sherburne, New York, following a touching, two-hour memorial celebration ... the longest service Reverend Steve had ever conducted. Nestled among the foothills of the Catskill Mountains, the intimate Columbus Community Church overflowed its 250-seat capacity with standing room only. More than thirty fraternity brothers stood shoulder to shoulder, lining the sidewalk while pallbearers carried their fallen brother past their ranks and into the church. It was an impressive and overwhelming sight.

Death is a part of life, but always more difficult to accept when it strikes the young. Memories must sustain us as we grieve our loss and rebuild our lives. To bury a child is a devastating experience.

During the ceremony so many people tearfully shared their fondest memories of Josh. Selecting the following poignant testimonials was a very difficult decision as I wanted to include them all. I derive great comfort and peace, knowing that Josh will remain forever embedded in our hearts.

Reflections ...

—*I never heard him say, "Why me?" I never heard him wail at God. The real definition of courage. He also redefined love for me. I come from a Webb[s]' ole English background, and we stand off in our love. Josh and I learned to hug and kiss and cry and say, "I love you" every day. I am very thankful for that. My beautiful daughter gave part of her body for him and gave so much support to him and he was mean to her. He wasn't perfect, but what a beautiful child! He would have fought on. He really wanted to live. We didn't give up. Technology gave up on us. I could not have been more proud of him for the lives he touched, the love he shared and the courage he possessed. As sure as I'm standing here with all the people I love, I know he's in heaven.* —Jim, proud father

*You are the sun in my heart and
I just want to hold you until I can't cry anymore.
I want to bring you from the dreadful waters and
Keep you safe here with me on the shore.
But you are free now,
As free as the sky and wind on your face.
So fly and soar, soar through the skies
And over mountains and across the seas
To the place where your heart can be at ease.
Where we can meet again and make a new start and
Live together forever and never have to say goodbye.
I love you forever and I am forever yours.* —Jody, fiancée

—Josh amazed everyone with his improbable survival many times. He appreciated the best of medical science and the healing arts both traditional and holistic. He was inspired by the strength and authority of nature. Certainly central to his survival was his delightful sense of humor. Another element to his survival was his grace. I'm sure he gets that from his grandfather, Leo. Josh was always so graceful and he had dignity no matter how naked he was or how bald he was, whether he was down in bed using a urinal or sitting in a wheelchair; whether mapped by the radiation marks or scarred by surgeons. He had dignity. —Judith, aunt and nurse

—Josh loved his gift to use the power of words to evoke the power of passion and love within people. He loved to make people laugh and cry. He wrote these words as the Man of Honor at my wedding which he entitled "The Wedding Poem." I believe we need to continue his legacy and love here in the physical world, living and loving everyday to the fullest, as Josh did, until we outgrow our physical shells and enter the spiritual world with Josh's soul, beautiful and loving, unconstrained by our fragile shells. —Kim, best friend and college classmate

A Wedding Poem for Kim and Jon
By Josh Webb

I have seen the fiery detail of dawn
Where the night embraces the day
Two becoming one; an awakening
Entangled unity of color
Calling to me
Alive, Alive
How I love thee
How I can feel the fiery detail of dusk
Where the day embraces the night
Two becoming one in slumber
Fading illuminations nestled on the rolling hills of the horizon
Like eyes closing, surrendering to touch
How I love thee
As the wanting sea dares to find the lonely land
And the lonely land reaches toward the wanting sea
And meets her sometimes in calm reflections
And at other times in passion's roaring fury
Always entwined at the shore
How I love thee
Two becoming one in a fire complete
Loneliness dispelled when loneliness meets
Beauty unfolding like a flower to the sun
Velvet lips enchanting, our love becoming one
Alive, Alive
How I love thee
How I fear being taken away
For the poet knows, the poet hears
The silent thunder of falling tears
When lovers, in death, are kept apart
From whisper, caress, and kindness of heart
And if life ever deems that I lose thee
I will defy this cruel decree
And I will meet you in the swirling light of dawn
On the shore where the land meets the sea.

—*I'll never forget the day. I remember it was a Sunday, the first part of March, and I got a phone call from Josh. He said, "Want to risk your life?" And I said, 'Sure. What are we doing?" So we proceeded to load the canoe up and canoed Little Pleasant Brook which usually has no water at all, but it was raging pretty good then. Of course, we tipped and we got cold but we had a great time. I've never known anyone more alive than Josh.* —Dave, friend

—*Josh and I lived next to each other the first year of college and were roommates for the next three years. What I will always remember about him is how he hurled himself through life and then sat down and told you a story about the adventure. There are stories perhaps we all know but there aren't many of us foolish enough to think you can parasail through a field behind a Ford Mustang, but the joy he got from that before the rope broke, and the joy I got from that, not even being there, but watching him tell that story and so many stories like it that I'm a part of. I will miss him as we all will.* —Will, roommate and fraternity brother

—*Josh changed my life in many ways. But the moment that I'll always remember when I think of Josh is when we were down on Kiawah Island ... I don't think I'd call it vacationing ... the Sig Pi fraternity brothers were all there ... it was a bit of a drinkfest; but one night we had stayed up all night and I was just lounging on the couch and Josh said to me, "Let's go down to the beach. I think the sun is rising." It wouldn't have occurred to me. So I said, "Sure, sure I'll go." And we stood there together just he and I. Friends don't really have to talk much to communicate and he just turned his head to me and said, ''Ominous!" The sun was coming up and the sea was in front of us and it was just that "ominous." I'm going to miss him. He was the only guy other than my father that I could hug, look him in the eye and say, "I love you."* —Mark, fraternity brother

Describing the poignant ceremony with personal reflections, two of Josh's fraternity brothers sent touching e-mails to those brothers unable to attend.

—*I was to be an usher at Josh's wedding to Jody. Instead I was a pallbearer at his funeral. Not the honor I would have preferred, but an honor nonetheless. All of us have memories of the times spent with Josh that were special to us. For me, the list of these memories is long and precious.*

These times were special because Josh was not only so very good with words, but also impressive unspoken. I have pictures in my mind of a look on his face knowing that he knew my thoughts and I his. It is a great loss that we can no longer look forward to the decades ahead with Josh, but we can look back on those special moments we have had. While we can no longer be blessed with Josh's presence, he will never really be gone. He is a part of us all. —Dave, fraternity brother

—I just got back from Sherburne, NY. Josh's funeral was awesome. I know that is a weird thing to say, but the love and support was so strong for Josh, his family and his friends that his death was no longer the focus. Josh got the royal treatment. We stood tall and basked in Josh's everlasting greatness. I cried and I laughed listening to the stories everyone shared. The wake was open casket. I wondered if I'd be freaked, but it turned out I was reassured. One look at his face and I found strength. He has that effect on many. The dude was a rock. Rob and I traveled to all his old hangouts. After all was said and done, Rob and I went back to Josh's grave. I had a few words with that old bastard. There he was resting comfortably in the ground, arms folded in complete peace. His grave covered with flowers. The dude was clearly styling. Death makes some things in life clearer. One thing is for sure—all that really matters is the love you share. Thanks for sharing yours, Josh! —Peter, fraternity brother

What great memories we all have of Josh! It was a deeply moving experience to witness the magnitude of love shared that day. I was overwhelmed. Love is timeless, forgiving and unrestricted by age. Love never dies.

* * *

Time has passed. The pain has not. I am so proud of my daughter, Julie, who has been a tremendous source of strength and comfort. She is my anchor. New bonds have emerged from the ashes of tragedy ... we are more than mother and daughter ... we are friends. I will always be extremely grateful to her for her unselfish bone marrow gift. She is a treasure as we struggle through our pain and begin anew.

Jody, with her childlike demeanor, never faltered as we combined our efforts to give Josh those extra years of quality life.

And when the chips were down and life was crumbling around us, Jim remained our beacon.

I still have great difficulty believing Josh is gone. Some days the flashbacks are so acute, so real I can smell the vomit and the antiseptic; hear the incessant beeping of the life support machines; feel the fear.

I will always treasure the joy Josh brought to my life and admire the strength and courage he possessed. I am grateful for the additional four years we shared as we, too, added a new dimension to our relationship. I was not only his mother, but his nurse, his care-giver, his optimism of restored health. Being able to care for him was my final gift of love.

Today, I take the days one at a time, relishing the uniqueness each has to offer, knowing life is so very short and tomorrow may never come.

∞

Thank you for your order!

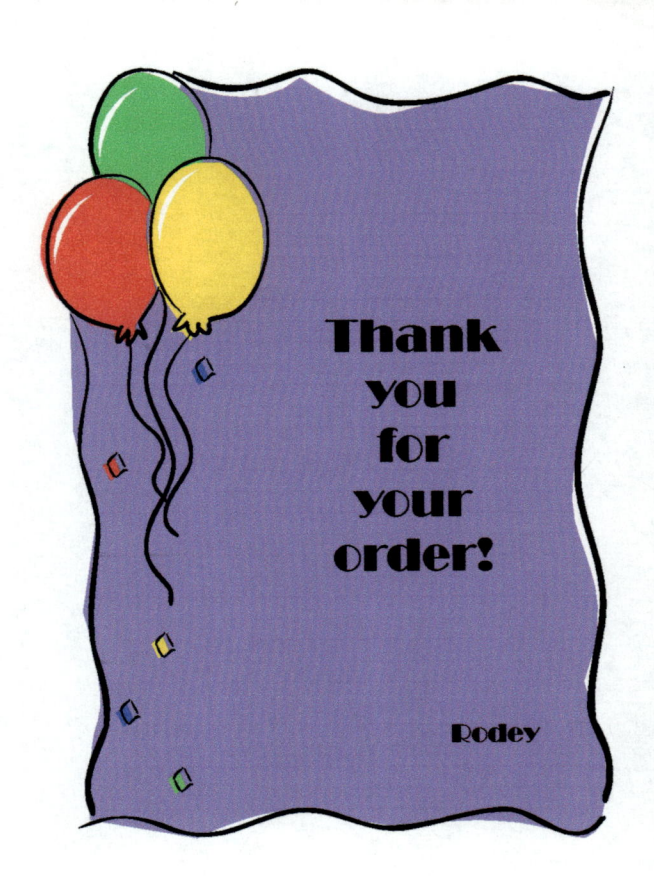

Rodey